Dear Reader,

There has never been a magical kingdom quite like Oz. Populated by good witches and wicked witches, wretched Nomes and enchanting princesses, chattering hens and cowardly lions—a whole host of marvelous creatures great and small and wise and wonderful—Oz is one of the most beloved fantasy worlds ever created.

The enormous explosion of all types of fantasy that we are seeing in today's market makes us feel that now is the time for a brilliantly successful Oz revival.

When we mention Oz to people who haven't grown up with the books, they nod, mention Judy Garland and think they know all there is to know about Oz. How wrong they are! They have no idea how rich the series is, how many wonderful characters and creatures there are. We have every expectation of making Oz as familiar to millions of fantasy readers as is Tolkien's Middle-earth and Lewis's Narnia.

Del Rey Books is now publishing the first seven books in the series, with more to follow.

Come, join us in Oz.

Magically,
Judy-Lynn & Lester del Rey
Del Rey Books

Oz IS . . .

"Oz—where the young stay young and the old grow young forever—these books are for readers of all ages."

—Ray Bradbury

"Who says the Land of Oz is only for the young? Age has nothing to do with it. Oz belongs to the young at heart and always will. All that is needed is an adventuresome spirit and a genuine affection for classic fantasy."

—Terry Brooks
Author of *The Sword of Shannara*

"I was raised with the Oz books, and their enchantment, humor and excitement remain with me. They are still a joy and a treasure. I welcome this Oz revival."

—Stephen R. Donaldson
Author of *The Chronicles of Thomas Covenant*

"The land of Oz has managed to fascinate each new generation . . . the Oz books continue to exert their spell . . . and those who read [them] are often made what they were not—imaginative, tolerant, alert to wonders, life."

—Gore Vidal
The New York Review of Books

THIS BOOK BELONGS
TO

The Wonderful Oz Books by L. Frank Baum
Now Published by Del Rey Books

*Coming Soon from Del Rey Books

THE ROAD TO OZ

In which is related how Dorothy Gale of Kansas,
The Shaggy Man, Button Bright, and Polychrome
the Rainbow's Daughter met on an
Enchanted Road and followed
it all the way to the
Marvelous Land
of Oz.

BY

L. FRANK BAUM

"Royal Historian of Oz"

ILLUSTRATED BY
JOHN R. NEILL

A Del Rey Book

BALLANTINE BOOKS • NEW YORK

A Del Rey Book
Published by Ballantine Books

"The Marvelous Land of Oz" Map Copyright © 1979 by
James E. Haff and Dick Martin. Reproduced by permission
of The International Wizard of Oz Club, Inc.

Library of Congress Catalog Card Number: 79-88480

ISBN 0-345-28227-2

This edition published by arrangement with Contemporary
Books, Inc.

Manufactured in the United States of America

First Ballantine Books Edition: November 1979

Cover art by Michael Herring

To My First Grandson

Joslyn Stanton Baum

T O MY READERS: Well, my dears, here is what you have asked for: another "Oz Book" about Dorothy's strange adventures. Toto is in this story, because you wanted him to be there, and many other characters which you will recognize are in the story, too. Indeed, the wishes of my little correspondents have been considered as carefully as possible, and if the story is not exactly as you would have written it yourselves, you must remember that a story has to be a story before it can be written down, and the writer cannot change it much without spoiling it.

In the preface to "Dorothy and the Wizard in Oz" I said I would like to write some stories that were not "Oz" stories, because I thought I had written about Oz long enough; but since that volume was published I have been fairly deluged with letters from children imploring me to "write more about Dorothy," and "more about Oz," and since I write only to please the children I shall try to respect their wishes.

There are some new characters in this book that ought to win your love. I'm very fond of the shaggy man myself, and I think you will like him, too. As for Polychrome—the

Rainbow's Daughter—and stupid little Button-Bright, they seem to have brought a new element of fun into these Oz stories, and I am glad I discovered them. Yet I am anxious to have you write and tell me how you like them.

Since this book was written I have received some very remarkable news from The Land of Oz, which has greatly astonished me. I believe it will astonish you, too, my dears, when you hear it. But it is such a long and exciting story that it must be saved for another book—and perhaps that book will be the last story that will ever be told about the Land of Oz.

L FRANK BAUM.

Coronado, 1909.

LIST OF CHAPTERS

THE ROAD TO OZ

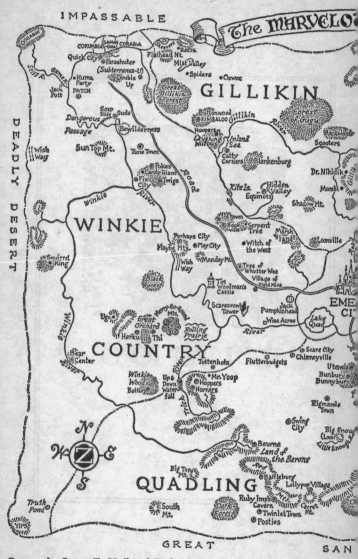

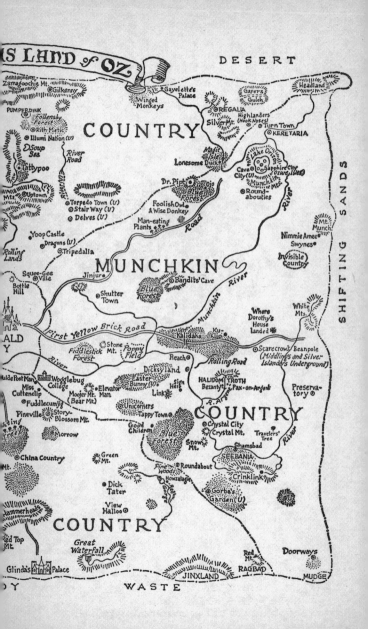

The Way to Butterfield

"PLEASE, miss," said the shaggy man, "can you tell me the road to Butterfield?"

Dorothy looked him over. Yes, he was shaggy, all right; but there was a twinkle in his eye that seemed pleasant.

"Oh, yes," she replied; "I can tell you. But it isn't this road at all."

"No?"

"You cross the ten-acre lot, follow the lane to the highway, go north to the five branches, and take—let me see—"

"To be sure, miss; see as far as Butterfield, if you like," said the shaggy man.

"You take the branch next the willow stump, I b'lieve; or else the branch by the gopher holes; or else——"

"Won't any of 'em do, miss?"

"'Course not, Shaggy Man. You must take the right road to get to Butterfield."

"And is that the one by the gopher stump, or——"

"Dear me!" cried Dorothy; "I shall have to show you the way; you're so stupid. Wait a minute till I run in the house and get my sun-bonnet."

The shaggy man waited. He had an oat-straw in his mouth, which he chewed slowly as if it tasted good; but it didn't. There was an apple-tree beside the house, and some apples had fallen to the ground. The shaggy man thought they would taste better than the oat-straw, so he walked over to get some. A little black dog with bright brown eyes dashed out of the farm-house and ran madly toward the shaggy man, who had already picked up three apples and put them in one of the big wide pockets of his shaggy coat. The little dog barked, and made a dive for the shaggy man's leg; but he grabbed the dog by the neck and put it in his big pocket along with the apples. He took more apples, afterward, for many were on the ground; and each one that he tossed into his pocket hit the little dog some-where upon the head or back, and made him growl. The little dog's name was Toto, and he

was sorry he had been put in the shaggy man's pocket.

Pretty soon Dorothy came out of the house with her sunbonnet, and she called out:

"Come on, Shaggy Man, if you want me to show you the road to Butterfield." She climbed the fence into the ten-acre lot and he followed her, walking slowly and stumbling over the little hillocks in the pasture as if he was thinking of something else and did not notice them.

"My, but you're clumsy!" said the little girl. "Are your feet tired?"

"No, miss; it's my whiskers; they tire very easily in this warm weather," said he. "I wish it would snow; don't you?"

" 'Course not, Shaggy Man," replied Dorothy,

giving him a severe look. "If it snowed in August it would spoil the corn and the oats and the wheat; and then Uncle Henry wouldn't have any crops; and that would make him poor; and——"

"Never mind," said the shaggy man. "It won't snow, I guess. Is this the lane?"

"Yes," replied Dorothy, climbing another fence; "I'll go as far as the highway with you."

"Thankee, miss; you're very kind for your size, I'm sure," said he gratefully.

"It isn't everyone who knows the road to Butterfield," Dorothy remarked as she tripped along the lane; "but I've driven there many a time with Uncle Henry, and so I b'lieve I could find it blindfolded."

"Don't do that, miss," said the shaggy man, earnestly; "you might make a mistake."

"I won't," she answered, laughing. "Here's the highway. Now, it's the second—no, the third turn to the left—or else it's the fourth. Let's see. The first one is by the elm tree; and the second is by the gopher holes; and then——"

"Then what?" he inquired, putting his hands in his coat pockets. Toto grabbed a finger and bit it; the shaggy man took his hand out of that pocket quickly, and said "Oh!"

Dorothy did not notice. She was shading her

eyes from the sun with her arm, looking anxiously down the road.

"Come on," she commanded. "It's only a little way farther, so I may as well show you."

After a while they came to the place where five roads branched in different directions; Dorothy pointed to one, and said:

"That's it, Shaggy Man."

"I'm much obliged, miss," he said, and started along another road.

"Not that one!" she cried; "you're going wrong."

He stopped.

"I thought you said that other was the road to Butterfield," said he, running his fingers through his shaggy whiskers in a puzzled way.

"So it is."

"But I don't want to go to Butterfield, miss."

"You don't?"

"Of course not. I wanted you to show me the road, so I shouldn't go there by mistake."

"Oh! Where *do* you want to go to, then?"

"I'm not particular, miss."

This answer astonished the little girl; and it made her provoked, too, to think she had taken all this trouble for nothing.

"There are a good many roads here," observed the shaggy man, turning slowly around, like a human windmill. "Seems to me a person could go 'most anywhere, from this place."

Dorothy turned around too, and gazed in surprise. There *were* a good many roads; more than she had ever seen before. She tried to count them, knowing there ought to be five; but when she had counted seventeen she grew bewildered and stopped, for the roads were as many as the spokes of a wheel and ran in every direction from the place where they stood; so if she kept on counting she was likely to count some of the roads twice.

"Dear me!" she exclaimed. "There used to be only five roads, highway and all. And now—why, where's the highway, Shaggy Man?"

"Can't say, miss," he responded, sitting down upon the ground as if tired with standing. "Wasn't it here a minute ago?"

"I thought so," she answered, greatly perplexed. "And I saw the gopher holes, too, and the dead stump; but they're not here now. These roads are all strange—and what a lot of them there are! Where do you suppose they all go to?"

"Roads," observed the shaggy man, "don't go anywhere. They stay in one place, so folks can walk on them."

He put his hand in his side-pocket and drew out an apple—quick, before Toto could bite him again. The little dog got his head out this time and said "Bow-wow!" so loudly that it made Dorothy jump.

"O, Toto!" she cried; "where did you come from?"

"I brought him along," said the shaggy man.

"What for?" she asked.

"To guard these apples in my pocket, miss, so no one would steal them."

With one hand the shaggy man held the apple, which he began eating, while with the other hand he pulled Toto out of his pocket and dropped him to the ground. Of course Toto made for Dorothy at once, barking joyfully at his release from the dark pocket. When the child had patted his head lovingly, he sat down before her, his red tongue hanging out one side of his mouth, and looked up into her face with his bright brown eyes, as if asking her what they should do next.

Dorothy didn't know. She looked around her anxiously for some familiar landmark; but everything was strange. Between the branches of the many roads were green meadows and a few shrubs and trees, but she couldn't see anywhere the farm-house from which she had just come, or anything she had ever seen before—except the shaggy man and Toto.

Besides this, she had turned around and around so many times, trying to find out where she was, that now she couldn't even tell which direction the farm-house ought to be in; and this began to worry her and make her feel anxious.

"I'm 'fraid, Shaggy Man," she said, with a sigh, "that we're lost!"

"That's nothing to be afraid of," he replied, throwing away the core of his apple and beginning to eat another one. "Each of these roads must lead somewhere, or it wouldn't be here. So what does it matter?"

"I want to go home again," she said.

"Well, why don't you?" said he.

"I don't know which road to take."

"That is too bad," he said, shaking his shaggy head gravely. "I wish I could help you; but I can't. I'm a stranger in these parts."

"Seems as if I were, too," she said, sitting down beside him. "It's funny. A few minutes ago I was home, and I just came to show you the way to Butterfield——"

"So I shouldn't make a mistake and go there——"

"And now I'm lost myself and don't know how to get home!"

"Have an apple," suggested the shaggy man, handing her one with pretty red cheeks.

"I'm not hungry," said Dorothy, pushing it away.

"But you may be, to-morrow; then you'll be sorry you didn't eat the apple," said he.

"If I am, I'll eat the apple then," promised Dorothy.

"Perhaps there won't be any apple then," he returned, beginning to eat the red-cheeked one himself. "Dogs sometimes can find their way home better than people," he went on; "perhaps your dog can lead you back to the farm."

"Will you, Toto?" asked Dorothy.

Toto wagged his tail vigorously.

"All right," said the girl; "let's go home."

Toto looked around a minute, and dashed up one of the roads.

"Good-bye, Shaggy Man," called Dorothy, and ran after Toto. The little dog pranced briskly along for some distance; then he turned around and looked at his mistress questioningly.

"Oh, don't 'spect *me* to tell you anything; I don't know the way," she said. "You'll have to find it yourself."

But Toto couldn't. He wagged his tail, and sneezed, and shook his ears, and trotted back where they had left the shaggy man. From here he started along another road; then came back and tried another; but each time he found the way strange and decided it would not take them to the farm-house. Finally, when Dorothy had begun to tire with chasing after him, Toto sat down panting beside the shaggy man and gave up.

Dorothy sat down, too, very thoughtful. The little girl had encountered some queer adventures since she came to live at the farm; but this was the queerest of them all. To get lost in fifteen minutes, so near to her home and in the unromantic State of Kansas, was an experience that fairly bewildered her.

"Will your folks worry?" asked the shaggy man, his eyes twinkling in a pleasant way.

"I s'pose so," answered Dorothy, with a sigh. "Uncle Henry says there's *always* something happening to me; but I've always come home safe at the last. So perhaps he'll take comfort and think I'll come home safe this time."

"I'm sure you will," said the shaggy man, smilingly nodding at her. "Good little girls never come to any harm, you know. For my part, I'm good, too; so nothing ever hurts me."

Dorothy looked at him curiously. His clothes were shaggy, his boots were shaggy and full of holes, and his hair and whiskers were shaggy. But his smile was sweet and his eyes were kind.

"Why didn't you want to go to Butterfield?" she asked.

"Because a man lives there who owes me fif-

"THIS, MY DEAR, IS THE WONDERFUL
LOVE MAGNET."

teen cents, and if I went to Butterfield and he saw me he'd want to pay me the money. I don't want money, my dear."

"Why not?" she inquired.

"Money," declared the shaggy man, "makes people proud and haughty; I don't want to be proud and haughty. All I want is to have people love me; and as long as I own the Love Magnet everyone I meet is sure to love me dearly."

"The Love Magnet! Why, what's that?"

"I'll show you, if you won't tell any one," he answered, in a low, mysterious voice.

"There isn't any one to tell, 'cept Toto," said the girl.

The shaggy man searched in one pocket, carefully; and in another pocket; and in a third. At last he drew out a small parcel wrapped in crumpled paper and tied with a cotton string. He unwound the string, opened the parcel, and took out a bit of metal shaped like a horseshoe. It was dull and brown, and not very pretty.

"This, my dear," said he, impressively, "is the wonderful Love Magnet. It was given me by an Eskimo in the Sandwich Islands—where there are no sandwiches at all—and as long as I carry it every living thing I meet will love me dearly."

"Why didn't the Eskimo keep it?" she asked, looking at the Magnet with interest.

"He got tired of being loved and longed for some one to hate him. So he gave me the Magnet and the very next day a grizzly bear ate him."

"Wasn't he sorry then?" she inquired.

"He didn't say," replied the shaggy man, wrapping and tying the Love Magnet with great care and putting it away in another pocket. "But the bear didn't seem sorry a bit," he added.

"Did you know the bear?" asked Dorothy.

"Yes; we used to play ball together in the Caviar Islands. The bear loved me because I had the Love Magnet. I couldn't blame him for eating the Eskimo, because it was his nature to do so."

"Once," said Dorothy, "I knew a Hungry Tiger who longed to eat fat babies, because it was his nature to; but he never ate any because he had a Conscience."

"This bear," replied the shaggy man, with a sigh, "had no Conscience, you see."

The shaggy man sat silent for several minutes, apparently considering the cases of the bear and the tiger, while Toto watched him with an air of great interest. The little dog was doubtless thinking of his ride in the shaggy man's pocket and planning to keep out of reach in the future.

At last the shaggy man turned and inquired, "What's your name, little girl?"

"My name's Dorothy," said she, jumping up again, "but what are we going to do? We can't stay here forever, you know."

"Let's take the seventh road," he suggested. "Seven is a lucky number for little girls named Dorothy."

"The seventh from where?"

"From where you begin to count."

So she counted seven roads, and the seventh looked just like all the others; but the shaggy man got up from the ground where he had been sitting and started down this road as if sure it was the best way to go; and Dorothy and Toto followed him.

Dorothy Meets Button-Bright

THE seventh road was a good road, and curved this way and that—winding through green meadows and fields covered with daisies and buttercups and past groups of shady trees. There were no houses of any sort to be seen, and for some distance they met with no living creature at all.

Dorothy began to fear they were getting a good way from the farm-house, since here everything was strange to her; but it would do no good at all to go back where the other roads all met, because the next one they chose might lead her just as far from home.

She kept on beside the shaggy man, who whistled cheerful tunes to beguile the journey, until by and by they followed a turn in the road and saw before them a big chestnut tree making a shady spot over the highway. In the shade sat a little boy dressed in sailor clothes, who was digging a hole in the earth with a bit of wood. He must have been digging some time, because the hole was already big enough to drop a football into.

Dorothy and Toto and the shaggy man came to a halt before the little boy, who kept on digging in a sober and persistent fashion.

"Who are you?" asked the girl.

He looked up at her calmly. His face was round and chubby and his eyes were big, blue, and earnest.

"I'm Button-Bright," said he.

"But what's your real name?" she inquired.

"Button-Bright."

"That isn't a really-truly name!" she exclaimed.

"Isn't it?" he asked, still digging.

" 'Course not. It's just a—a thing to call you by. You must have a name."

"Must I?"

"To be sure. What does your mamma call you?"

He paused in his digging and tried to think.

"Papa always said I was bright as a button; so mamma always called me Button-Bright," he said.

"What is your papa's name?"

"Just Papa."

"What else?"

"Don't know."

"Never mind," said the shaggy man, smiling. "We'll call the boy Button-Bright, as his mamma does. That name is as good as any, and better than some."

Dorothy watched the boy dig.

"Where do you live?" she asked.

"Don't know," was the reply.

"How did you come here?"

"Don't know," he said again.

"Don't you know where you came from?"

"No," said he.

"Why, he must be lost," she said to the shaggy man. She turned to the boy once more.

"What are you going to do?" she inquired.

"Dig," said he.

"But you can't dig forever; and what are you going to do then?" she persisted.

"Don't know," said the boy.

"But you *must* know *something*," declared Dorothy, getting provoked.

"Must I?" he asked, looking up in surprise.

"Of course you must."

"What must I know?"

"What's going to become of you, for one thing," she answered.

"Do *you* know what's going to become of me?" he asked.

"Not—not 'zactly," she admitted.

"Do you know what's going to become of *you?*" he continued, earnestly.

"I can't say I do," replied Dorothy, remembering her present difficulties.

The shaggy man laughed.

"No one knows everything, Dorothy," he said.

"But Button-Bright doesn't seem to know *any*-thing," she declared. "Do you, Button-Bright?"

He shook his head, which had pretty curls all over it, and replied with perfect calmness:

"Don't know."

Never before had Dorothy met with anyone who could give her so little information. The boy was evidently lost, and his people would be sure to worry about him. He seemed two or three years younger than Dorothy, and was prettily dressed, as if some one loved him dearly and took much pains to make him look well. How, then, did he come to be in this lonely road? she wondered.

Near Button-Bright, on the ground, lay a sailor hat with a gilt anchor on the band. His sailor trousers were long and wide at the bottom, and the broad collar of his blouse had gold anchors sewed on its corners. The boy was still digging at his hole.

"Have you ever been to sea?" asked Dorothy.

"To see what?" answered Button-Bright.

"I mean have you ever been where there's water?"

"Yes," said Button-Bright; "there's a well in our back yard."

"You don't understand," cried Dorothy. "I mean, have you ever been on a big ship floating on a big ocean?"

"Don't know," said he.

"Then why do you wear sailor clothes?"

"Don't know," he answered, again.

Dorothy was in despair.

"You're just *awful* stupid, Button-Bright," she said.

"Am I?" he asked.

"Yes, you are."

"Why?" looking up at her with big eyes.

She was going to say: "Don't know," but stopped herself in time.

"That's for you to answer," she replied.

"It's no use asking Button-Bright questions," said the shaggy man, who had been eating another apple; "but some one ought to take care of the poor little chap, don't you think? So he'd better come along with us."

Toto had been looking with great curiosity into the hole which the boy was digging, and growing more and more excited every minute, perhaps thinking that Button-Bright was after some wild animal. The little dog began barking loudly and jumped into the hole himself, where he began to dig with his tiny paws, making the earth fly in all directions. It spattered over the boy. Dorothy seized him and raised him to his feet, brushing his clothes with her hand.

"Stop that, Toto!" she called. "There aren't any mice or woodchucks in that hole, so don't be foolish."

Toto stopped, sniffed at the hole suspiciously, and jumped out of it, wagging his tail as if he had done something important.

"Well," said the shaggy man, "let's start on, or we won't get anywhere before night comes."

"Where do you expect to get to?" asked Dorothy.

"I'm like Button-Bright; I don't know," answered the shaggy man, with a laugh. "But I've learned from long experience that every road leads somewhere, or there wouldn't be any road; so it's likely that if we travel long enough, my dear, we will come to some place or another in the end. What place it will be we can't even guess at this moment, but we're sure to find out when we get there."

"Why, yes," said Dorothy; "that seems reas'n-'ble, Shaggy Man."

A Queer Village

BUTTON-BRIGHT took the shaggy man's hand willingly; for the shaggy man had the Love Magnet, you know, which was the reason Button-Bright had loved him at once. They started on, with Dorothy on one side, and Toto on the other, the little party trudging along more cheerfully than you might have supposed. The girl was getting used to queer adventures, which interested her very much. Wherever Dorothy went Toto was sure to go, like Mary's little lamb. Button-Bright didn't seem a bit afraid or worried because he was lost, and the shaggy man had no home, perhaps, and was as happy in one place as in another.

Before long they saw ahead of them a fine big arch spanning the road, and when they came nearer they found that the arch was beautifully carved and decorated with rich colors. A row of peacocks with spread tails ran along the top of it, and all the feathers were gorgeously painted. In the center was a large fox's head, and the fox wore a shrewd and knowing expression and had large spectacles over its eyes and a small golden crown with shiny points on top of its head.

While the travelers were looking with curiosity at this beautiful arch there suddenly marched out of it a company of soldiers—only the soldiers were all foxes dressed in uniforms. They wore green jackets and yellow pantaloons, and their little round caps and their high boots were a bright red color. Also there was a big red bow tied about the middle of each long, bushy tail. Each soldier was armed with a wooden sword having an edge of sharp teeth set in a row, and the sight of these teeth at first caused Dorothy to shudder.

A captain marched in front of the company of fox-soldiers, his uniform embroidered with gold braid to make it handsomer than the others.

Almost before our friends realized it the soldiers had surrounded them on all sides, and the captain was calling out in a harsh voice:

"Surrender! You are our prisoners."

"What's a pris'ner?" asked Button-Bright.

"A prisoner is a captive," replied the fox-captain, strutting up and down with much dignity.

"What's a captive?" asked Button-Bright.

"You're one," said the captain.

That made the shaggy man laugh.

"Good afternoon, captain," he said, bowing politely to all the foxes and very low to their commander. "I trust you are in good health, and that your families are all well?"

The fox-captain looked at the shaggy man, and his sharp features grew pleasant and smiling.

"We're pretty well, thank you, Shaggy Man," said he; and Dorothy knew that the Love Magnet was working and that all the foxes now loved the shaggy man because of it. But Toto didn't know this, for he began barking angrily and tried to bite the captain's hairy leg where it showed between his red boots and his yellow pantaloons.

"Stop, Toto!" cried the little girl, seizing the dog in her arms. "These are our friends."

"Why, so we are!" remarked the captain in tones of astonishment. "I thought at first we were enemies, but it seems you are friends, instead. You must come with me to see King Dox."

"Who's he?" asked Button-Bright, with earnest eyes.

"King Dox of Foxville; the great and wise sovereign who rules over our community."

"What's sov'rin, and what's c'u'nity?" inquired Button-Bright.

"Don't ask so many questions, little boy."

"Why?"

"Ah, why, indeed?" exclaimed the captain, looking at Button-Bright admiringly. "If you don't ask questions you will learn nothing. True enough. I was wrong. You're a very clever little boy, come to think of it—very clever indeed. But now, friends, please come with me, for it is my duty to escort you at once to the royal palace."

The soldiers marched back through the arch again, and with them marched the shaggy man, Dorothy, Toto, and Button-Bright. Once through the opening they found a fine, big city spread out before them, all the houses of carved marble in beautiful colors. The decorations were mostly birds and other fowl, such as peacocks, pheasants, turkeys, prairie-chickens, ducks, and geese. Over each doorway was carved a head representing the fox who lived in that house, this effect being quite pretty and unusual.

As our friends marched along, some of the foxes came out on the porches and balconies to get a view of the strangers. These foxes were all handsomely dressed, the girl-foxes and women-foxes wearing gowns of feathers woven together effectively and colored in bright hues which Dorothy thought were quite artistic and decidedly attractive.

Button-Bright stared until his eyes were big and round, and he would have stumbled and fallen more than once had not the shaggy man grasped his hand tightly. They were all interested, and Toto was so excited he wanted to bark every minute and to chase and fight every fox he caught sight of; but Dorothy held his little wiggling body fast in her arms and commanded him to be good and behave himself. So he finally quieted down, like a wise doggy, deciding there were too many foxes in Foxville to fight at one time.

By-and-by they came to a big square, and in

the center of the square stood the royal palace. Dorothy knew it at once because it had over its great door the carved head of a fox just like the one she had seen on the arch, and this fox was the only one who wore a golden crown.

There were many fox-soldiers guarding the door, but they bowed to the captain and admitted him without question. The captain led them through many rooms, where richly dressed foxes were sitting on beautiful chairs or sipping tea, which was being passed around by fox-servants in white aprons. They came to a big doorway covered with heavy curtains of cloth of gold.

Beside this doorway stood a huge drum. The fox-captain went to this drum and knocked his knees against it—first one knee and then the other—so that the drum said: "Boom-boom."

"You must all do exactly what I do," ordered the captain; so the shaggy man pounded the drum with his knees, and so did Dorothy and so did Button-Bright. The boy wanted to keep on pounding it with his little fat knees, because he liked the sound of it; but the captain stopped him. Toto couldn't pound the drum with his knees and he didn't know enough to wag his tail against it, so Dorothy pounded the drum for him and that made him bark, and when the little dog barked the fox-captain scowled.

The golden curtains drew back far enough to make an opening, through which marched the captain with the others.

The broad, long room they entered was decorated in gold with stained-glass windows of splendid colors. In the center of the room, upon a richly carved golden throne, sat the fox-king, surrounded by a group of other foxes, all of whom wore great spectacles over their eyes, making them look solemn and important.

Dorothy knew the King at once, because she had seen his head carved on the arch and over the doorway of the palace. Having met with several other kings in her travels she knew what to do, and at once made a low bow before the throne. The shaggy man bowed, too, and Button-Bright bobbed his head and said "Hello."

"Most wise and noble Potentate of Foxville," said the captain, addressing the King in a pompous voice, "I humbly beg to report that I found these strangers on the road leading to your Foxy Majesty's dominions, and have therefore brought them before you, as is my duty."

"So—so," said the King, looking at them keenly. "What brought you here, strangers?"

"Our legs, may it please your Royal Hairiness," replied the shaggy man.

"What is your business here?" was the next question.

"To get away as soon as possible," said the shaggy man.

The King didn't know about the Magnet, of course; but it made him love the shaggy man at once.

"Do just as you please about going away," he said; "but I'd like to show you the sights of my city and to entertain your party while you are here. We feel highly honored to have little Dorothy with us, I assure you, and we appreciate her kindness in making us a visit. For whatever country Dorothy visits is sure to become famous."

This speech greatly surprised the little girl, who asked:

"How did your Majesty know my name?"

"Why, everybody knows you, my dear," said

the Fox-King. "Don't you realize that? You are quite an important personage since Princess Ozma of Oz made you her friend."

"Do you know Ozma?" she asked, wondering.

"I regret to say that I do not," he answered, sadly; "but I hope to meet her soon. You know the Princess Ozma is to celebrate her birthday on the twenty-first of this month."

"Is she?" said Dorothy. "I didn't know that."

"Yes; it is to be the most brilliant royal ceremony ever held in any city in Fairyland, and I hope you will try to get me an invitation."

Dorothy thought a moment.

"I'm sure Ozma would invite you if I asked her," she said; "but how could you get to the Land of Oz and the Emerald City? It's a good way from Kansas."

"Kansas!" he exclaimed, surprised.

"Why, yes; we are in Kansas now, aren't we?" she returned.

"What a queer notion!" cried the Fox-King, beginning to laugh. "Whatever made you think this is Kansas?"

"I left Uncle Henry's farm only about two hours ago; that's the reason," she said, rather perplexed.

"But, tell me, my dear, did you ever see so wonderful a city as Foxville in Kansas?" he questioned.

"No, your Majesty."

"And haven't you traveled from Oz to Kansas in less than half a jiffy, by means of the Silver Shoes and the Magic Belt?"

"Yes, your Majesty," she acknowledged.

"Then why do you wonder that an hour or two could bring you to Foxville, which is nearer to Oz than it is to Kansas?"

"Dear me!" exclaimed Dorothy; "is this another fairy adventure?"

"It seems to be," said the Fox-King, smiling.

Dorothy turned to the shaggy man, and her face was grave and reproachful.

"Are you a magician? or a fairy in disguise?" she asked. "Did you enchant me when you asked the way to Butterfield?"

The shaggy man shook his head.

"Who ever heard of a shaggy fairy?" he replied. "No, Dorothy, my dear; I'm not to blame for this journey in any way, I assure you. There's been something strange about me ever since I owned the Love Magnet; but I don't know what it is any more than you do. I didn't try to get you away from home, at all. If you want to find your way back to the farm I'll go with you willingly, and do my best to help you."

"Never mind," said the little girl, thoughtfully. "There isn't so much to see in Kansas as there is here, and I guess Aunt Em won't be *very* much worried; that is, if I don't stay away too long."

"That's right," declared the Fox-King, nodding approval. "Be contented with your lot,

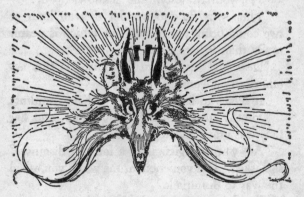

HIS ROYAL FOXINESS

whatever it happens to be, if you are wise. Which reminds me that you have a new companion on this adventure—he looks very clever and bright."

"He is," said Dorothy; and the shaggy man added:

"That's his name, your Royal Foxiness—Button-Bright."

King Dox

IT was amusing to note the expression on the face of King Dox as he looked the boy over, from his sailor hat to his stubby shoes; and it was equally diverting to watch Button-Bright stare at the King in return. No fox ever beheld a fresher, fairer child's face, and no child had ever before heard a fox talk, or met with one who dressed so handsomely and ruled so big a city. I am sorry to say that no one had ever told the little boy much about fairies of any kind; this being the case, it is easy to understand how much this strange experience startled and astonished him.

"How do you like us?" asked the King.

"Don't know," said Button-Bright.

"Of course you don't. It's too short an acquaintance," returned his Majesty. "What do you suppose my name is?"

"Don't know," said Button-Bright.

"How should you? Well, I'll tell you. My private name is Dox, but a King can't be called by his private name; he has to take one that is official. Therefore my official name is King Renard the Fourth. Ren-ard with the accent on the 'Ren'."

"What's 'ren'?" asked Button-Bright.

"How clever!" exclaimed the King, turning a pleased face toward his counselors. "This boy is indeed remarkably bright. 'What's 'ren'?' he asks; and of course 'ren' is nothing at all, all by itself. Yes; he's very bright indeed."

"That question is what your Majesty might call foxy," said one of the counselors, an old grey fox.

"So it is," declared the King. Turning again to Button-Bright, he asked:

"Having told you my name, what would you call me?"

"King Dox," said the boy.

"Why?"

" 'Cause 'ren' 's nothing at all," was the reply.

"Good! Very good indeed! You certainly have a brilliant mind. Do you know why two and two make four?"

"No," said Button-Bright.

"Clever! clever indeed. Of course you don't know. Nobody knows why; we only know it's so, and can't tell why it's so. Button-Bright, those curls and blue eyes do not go well with so much wisdom. They make you look too youthful, and hide your real cleverness. Therefore, I will do you a great favor. I will confer upon you the

head of a fox, so that you may hereafter look as bright as you really are."

As he spoke the King waved his paw toward the boy, and at once the pretty curls and fresh round face and big blue eyes were gone, while in their place a fox's head appeared upon Button-Bright's shoulders—a hairy head with a sharp nose, pointed ears, and keen little eyes.

"Oh, don't do that!" cried Dorothy, shrinking

36

back from her transformed companion with a
shocked and dismayed face.

"Too late, my dear; it's done. But you also
shall have a fox's head if you can prove you're
as clever as Button-Bright."

"I don't want it; it's dreadful!" she exclaimed;
and, hearing this verdict, Button-Bright began
to boo-hoo just as if he were still a little boy.

"How can you call that lovely head dreadful?"
asked the King. "It's a much prettier face than
he had before, to my notion, and my wife says
I'm a good judge of beauty. Don't cry, little fox-
boy. Laugh and be proud, because you are so
highly favored. How do you like the new head,
Button-Bright?"

"D-d-don't n-n-n-know!" sobbed the child.

"Please, *please* change him back again, your
Majesty!" begged Dorothy.

King Renard IV shook his head.

"I can't do that," he said; "I haven't the power,
even if I wanted to. No, Button-Bright must
wear his fox head, and he'll be sure to love it
dearly as soon as he gets used to it."

Both the shaggy man and Dorothy looked
grave and anxious, for they were sorrowful that
such a misfortune had overtaken their little companion. Toto barked at the fox-boy once or twice,
not realizing it was his former friend who now

wore the animal head; but Dorothy cuffed the dog and made him stop. As for the foxes, they all seemed to think Button-Bright's new head very becoming and that their King had conferred a great honor on this little stranger.

It was funny to see the boy reach up to feel of his sharp nose and wide mouth, and wail afresh with grief. He wagged his ears in a comical manner and tears were in his little black eyes. But Dorothy couldn't laugh at her friend just yet, because she felt so sorry.

Just then three little fox-princesses, daughters of the King, entered the room, and when they saw Button-Bright one exclaimed: "How lovely he is!" and the next one cried in delight: "How sweet he is!" and the third princess clapped her hands with pleasure and said, "How beautiful he is!"

Button-Bright stopped crying and asked timidly:

"Am I?"

"In all the world there is not another face so pretty," declared the biggest fox-princess.

"You must live with us always, and be our brother," said the next.

"We shall all love you dearly," the third said.

This praise did much to comfort the boy, and he looked around and tried to smile. It was a pitiful attempt, because the fox face was new and stiff, and Dorothy thought his expression more stupid than before the transformation.

"I think we ought to be going now," said the shaggy man, uneasily, for he didn't know what the King might take into his head to do next.

"Don't leave us yet, I beg of you," pleaded King Renard. "I intend to have several days of feasting and merry-making, in honor of your visit."

"Have it after we're gone, for we can't wait," said Dorothy, decidedly. But seeing this displeased the King, she added: "If I'm going to get Ozma to invite you to her party I'll have to find her as soon as poss'ble, you know."

In spite of all the beauty of Foxville and the gorgeous dresses of its inhabitants, both the girl and the shaggy man felt they were not quite safe there, and would be glad to see the last of it.

"But it is now evening," the King reminded them, "and you must stay with us until morning, anyhow. Therefore I invite you to be my guests at dinner, and to attend the theater afterward and sit in the royal box. To-morrow morning, if you really insist upon it, you may resume your journey."

They consented to this, and some of the fox-servants led them to a suite of lovely rooms in the big palace.

Button-Bright was afraid to be left alone, so

Dorothy took him into her own room. While a maid-fox dressed the little girl's hair—which was a bit tangled—and put some bright, fresh ribbons in it, another maid-fox combed the hair on poor Button-Bright's face and head and brushed it carefully, tying a pink bow to each of his pointed ears. The maids wanted to dress the children in fine costumes of woven feathers, such as all the foxes wore; but neither of them consented to that.

"A sailor suit and a fox head do not go well together," said one of the maids; "for no fox was ever a sailor that I can remember."

"I'm not a fox!" cried Button-Bright.

"Alas, no," agreed the maid. "But you've got a lovely fox head on your skinny shoulders, and that's *almost* as good as being a fox."

The boy, reminded of his misfortune, began to cry again. Dorothy petted and comforted him and promised to find some way to restore him his own head.

"If we can manage to get to Ozma," she said, "the Princess will change you back to yourself in half a second; so you just wear that fox head as comf't'bly as you can, dear, and don't worry about it at all. It isn't nearly as pretty as your own head, no matter what the foxes say; but you can get along with it for a little while longer, can't you?"

"Don't know," said Button-Bright, doubtfully; but he didn't cry any more after that.

Dorothy let the maids pin ribbons to her shoulders, after which they were ready for the King's dinner. When they met the shaggy man in the splendid drawing-room of the palace they found him just the same as before. He had re-fused to give up his shaggy clothes for new ones, because if he did that he would no longer be the shaggy man, he said, and he might have to get acquainted with himself all over again.

He told Dorothy he had brushed his shaggy hair and whiskers; but she thought he must have brushed them the wrong way, for they were quite as shaggy as before.

As for the company of foxes assembled to

dine with the strangers, they were most beautifully costumed, and their rich dresses made Dorothy's simple gown and Button-Bright's sailor suit and the shaggy man's shaggy clothes look commonplace. But they treated their guests with great respect and the King's dinner was a very good dinner indeed.

Foxes, as you know, are fond of chicken and other fowl; so they served chicken soup and roasted turkey and stewed duck and fried grouse and broiled quail and goose pie, and as the cooking was excellent the King's guests enjoyed the meal and ate heartily of the various dishes.

The party went to the theater, where they saw a play acted by foxes dressed in costumes of brilliantly colored feathers. The play was about a fox-girl who was stolen by some wicked wolves and carried to their cave; and just as they were about to kill her and eat her a company of fox-soldiers marched up, saved the girl, and put all the wicked wolves to death.

"How do you like it?" the King asked Dorothy.

"Pretty well," she answered. "It reminds me of one of Mr. Aesop's fables."

"Don't mention Aesop to me, I beg of you!" exclaimed King Dox. "I hate that man's name. He wrote a good deal about foxes, but always

made them out cruel and wicked, whereas we are gentle and kind, as you may see."

"But his fables showed you to be wise and clever, and more shrewd than other animals," said the shaggy man, thoughtfully.

"So we are. There is no question about our knowing more than men do," replied the King, proudly. "But we employ our wisdom to do good, instead of harm; so that horrid Aesop did not know what he was talking about."

They did not like to contradict him, because they felt he ought to know the nature of foxes better than men did; so they sat still and watched the play, and Button-Bright became so interested that for the time he forgot he wore a fox head.

Afterward they went back to the palace and slept in soft beds stuffed with feathers; for the foxes raised many fowl for food, and used their feathers for clothing and to sleep upon.

Dorothy wondered why the animals living in Foxville did not wear just their own hairy skins, as wild foxes do; when she mentioned it to King Dox he said they clothed themselves because they were civilized.

"But you were born without clothes," she observed, "and you don't seem to me to need them."

"So were human beings born without clothes," he replied; "and until they became civilized they wore only their natural skins. But to become civilized means to dress as elaborately and prettily as possible, and to make a show of your clothes so your neighbors will envy you, and for that reason both civilized foxes and civilized humans spend most of their time dressing themselves."

"I don't," declared the shaggy man.

"That is true," said the King, looking at him carefully; "but perhaps you are not civilized."

After a sound sleep and a good night's rest they had their breakfast with the King and then bade his Majesty good-bye.

"You've been kind to us—'cept poor Button-Bright," said Dorothy, "and we've had a nice time in Foxville."

"Then," said King Dox, "perhaps you'll be

good enough to get me an invitation to Princess Ozma's birthday celebration."

"I'll try," she promised; "if I see her in time."

"It's on the twenty-first, remember," he continued; "and if you'll just see that I'm invited I'll find a way to cross the Dreadful Desert into the marvelous Land of Oz. I've always wanted to visit the Emerald City, so I'm sure it was fortunate you arrived here just when you did, you being Princess Ozma's friend and able to assist me in getting the invitation."

"If I see Ozma I'll ask her to invite you," she replied.

The Fox-King had a delightful luncheon put up for them, which the shaggy man shoved in his pocket, and the fox-captain escorted them to an arch at the side of the village opposite the one by which they had entered. Here they found more soldiers guarding the road.

"Are you afraid of enemies?" asked Dorothy.

"No; because we are watchful and able to protect ourselves," answered the captain. "But this road leads to another village peopled by big, stupid beasts who might cause us trouble if they thought we were afraid of them."

"What beasts are they?" asked the shaggy man.

The captain hesitated to answer. Finally he said:

"You will learn all about them when you arrive at their city. But do not be afraid of them. Button-Bright is so wonderfully clever and has now such an intelligent face that I'm sure he will manage to find a way to protect you."

This made Dorothy and the shaggy man rather uneasy, for they had not so much confidence in the fox-boy's wisdom as the captain seemed to have. But as their escort would say no more about the beasts, they bade him goodbye and proceeded on their journey.

The Rainbow's Daughter

TOTO, now allowed to run about as he pleased, was glad to be free again and able to bark at the birds and chase the butterflies. The country around them was charming, yet in the pretty fields of wild-flowers and groves of leafy trees were no houses whatever, or sign of any inhabitants. Birds flew through the air and cunning white rabbits darted amongst the tall grasses and green bushes; Dorothy noticed even the ants toiling busily along the roadway, bearing gigantic loads of clover seed; but of people there were none at all.

They walked briskly on for an hour or two, for even little Button-Bright was a good walker and did not tire easily. At length as they turned

a curve in the road they beheld just before them
a curious sight.

A little girl, radiant and beautiful, shapely as
a fairy and exquisitely dressed, was dancing
gracefully in the middle of the lonely road,
whirling slowly this way and that, her dainty
feet twinkling in sprightly fashion. She was clad
in flowing, fluffy robes of soft material that reminded Dorothy of woven cobwebs, only it was
colored in soft tintings of violet, rose, topaz, olive,
azure, and white, mingled together most har-
moniously in stripes which melted one into the
other with soft blendings. Her hair was like spun
gold and floated around her in a cloud, no strand
being fastened or confined by either pin or ornament or ribbon.

Filled with wonder and admiration our friends
approached and stood watching this fascinating
dance. The girl was no taller than Dorothy, although more slender; nor did she seem any older
than our little heroine.

Suddenly she paused and abandoned the
dance, as if for the first time observing the
presence of strangers. As she faced them, shy as
a frightened fawn, poised upon one foot as if to
fly the next instant, Dorothy was astonished to
see tears flowing from her violet eyes and trick-
ling down her lovely rose-hued cheeks. That the

POLYCHROME—THE RAINBOW'S DAUGHTER

dainty maiden should dance and weep at the same time was indeed surprising; so Dorothy asked in a soft, sympathetic voice:

"Are you unhappy, little girl?"

"Very!" was the reply; "I am lost."

"Why, so are we," said Dorothy, smiling; "but we don't cry about it."

"Don't you? Why not?"

" 'Cause I've been lost before, and always got found again," answered Dorothy, simply.

"But I've never been lost before," murmured the dainty maiden, "and I'm worried and afraid."

"You were dancing," remarked Dorothy, in a puzzled tone of voice.

"Oh, that was just to keep warm," explained the maiden, quickly. "It was not because I felt happy or gay, I assure you."

Dorothy looked at her closely. Her gauzy flowing robes might not be very warm, yet the weather wasn't at all chilly, but rather mild and balmy, like a spring day.

"Who are you, dear?" she asked, gently.

"I'm Polychrome," was the reply.

"Polly whom?"

"Polychrome. I'm the Daughter of the Rainbow."

"Oh!" said Dorothy, with a gasp; "I didn't know the Rainbow had children. But I *might* have known it, before you spoke. You couldn't really be anything else."

"Why not?" inquired Polychrome, as if surprised.

"Because you're so lovely and sweet."

The little maiden smiled through her tears, came up to Dorothy, and placed her slender fingers in the Kansas girl's chubby hand.

"You'll be my friend—won't you?" she said, pleadingly.

"Of course."

"And what is your name?"

"I'm Dorothy; and this is my friend Shaggy Man, who owns the Love Magnet; and this is Button-Bright—only you don't see him as he really is because the Fox-King carelessly changed his head into a fox head. But the real Button-Bright is good to look at, and I hope to get him changed back to himself, some time."

The Rainbow's Daughter nodded cheerfully, no longer afraid of her new companions.

"But who is this?" she asked, pointing to Toto, who was sitting before her wagging his tail in the most friendly manner and admiring the pretty maid with his bright eyes. "Is this, also, some enchanted person?"

"Oh no, Polly—I may call you Polly, mayn't I? Your whole name's awful hard to say."

"Call me Polly if you wish, Dorothy."

"Well, Polly, Toto's just a dog; but he has more sense than Button-Bright, to tell the truth; and I'm very fond of him."

"So am I," said Polychrome, bending gracefully to pat Toto's head.

"But how did the Rainbow's Daughter ever get on this lonely road, and become lost?" asked the shaggy man, who had listened wonderingly to all this.

"Why, my father stretched his rainbow over here this morning, so that one end of it touched this road," was the reply; "and I was dancing upon the pretty rays, as I love to do, and never noticed I was getting too far over the bend in the circle. Suddenly I began to slide, and I went faster and faster until at last I bumped on the ground, at the very end. Just then father lifted the rainbow again, without noticing me at all, and though I tried to seize the end of it and hold fast, it melted away entirely and I was left alone and helpless on the cold, hard earth!"

"It doesn't seem cold to me, Polly," said Dorothy; "but perhaps you're not warmly dressed."

"I'm so used to living nearer the sun," replied the Rainbow's Daughter, "that at first I feared I would freeze down here. But my dance has warmed me some, and now I wonder how I am ever to get home again."

"Won't your father miss you, and look for you, and let down another rainbow for you?"

"Perhaps so; but he's busy just now because it rains in so many parts of the world at this season,

and he has to set his rainbow in a lot of different places. What would you advise me to do, Dorothy?"

"Come with us," was the answer. "I'm going to try to find my way to the Emerald City, which is in the fairy Land of Oz. The Emerald City is ruled by a friend of mine, the Princess Ozma, and if we can manage to get there I'm sure she will know a way to send you home to your father again."

"Do you really think so?" asked Polychrome, anxiously.

"I'm pretty sure."

"Then I'll go with you," said the little maid; "for travel will help keep me warm, and father can find me in one part of the world as well as another—if he gets time to look for me."

"Come along, then," said the shaggy man, cheerfully; and they started on once more. Polly walked beside Dorothy a while, holding her new friend's hand as if she feared to let it go; but her nature seemed as light and buoyant as her fleecy robes, for suddenly she darted ahead and whirled round in a giddy dance. Then she tripped back to them with sparkling eyes and smiling cheeks, having regained her usual happy mood and forgotten all her worry about being lost.

They found her a charming companion, and

her dancing and laughter—for she laughed at times like the tinkling of a silver bell—did much to enliven their journey and keep them contented.

The City of Beasts

WHEN noon came they opened the Fox-King's basket of luncheon, and found a nice roasted turkey with cranberry sauce and some slices of bread and butter. As they sat on the grass by the roadside the shaggy man cut up the turkey with his pocket-knife and passed slices of it around.

"Haven't you any dewdrops, or mist-cakes, or cloudbuns?" asked Polychrome, longingly.

"Course not," replied Dorothy. "We eat solid things, down here on the earth. But there's a bottle of cold tea. Try some, won't you?"

The Rainbow's Daughter watched Button-Bright devour one leg of the turkey.

"Is it good?" she asked.

He nodded.

"Do you think I could eat it?"

"Not this," said Button-Bright.

"But I mean another piece?"

"Don't know," he replied.

"Well, I'm going to try, for I'm very hungry," she decided, and took a thin slice of the white breast of turkey which the shaggy man cut for her, as well as a bit of bread and butter. When she tasted it Polychrome thought the turkey was good—better even than mist-cakes; but a little satisfied her hunger and she finished with a tiny sip of cold tea.

"That's about as much as a fly would eat," said Dorothy, who was making a good meal herself. "But I know some people in Oz who eat nothing at all."

"Who are they?" inquired the shaggy man.

"One is a scarecrow who's stuffed with straw, and the other a woodman made out of tin. They haven't any appetites inside of 'em, you see; so they never eat anything at all."

"Are they alive?" asked Button-Bright.

"Oh yes," replied Dorothy; "and they're very clever and very nice, too. If we get to Oz I'll introduce them to you."

"Do you really expect to get to Oz?" inquired the shaggy man, taking a drink of cold tea.

"I don't know just what to 'spect," answered the child, seriously; "but I've noticed if I hap-

POLLY SIPPED A LITTLE COLD TEA

pen to get lost I'm almost sure to come to the
Land of Oz in the end, somehow 'r other; so I
may get there this time. But I can't promise, you
know; all I can do is wait and see."

"Will the Scarecrow scare me?" asked Button-
Bright.

"No; 'cause you're not a crow," she returned.
"He has the loveliest smile you ever saw—only
it's painted on and he can't help it."

Luncheon being over they started again upon
their journey, the shaggy man, Dorothy and
Button-Bright walking soberly along, side by
side, and the Rainbow's Daughter dancing merrily before them.

Sometimes she darted along the road so swiftly
that she was nearly out of sight, then she came
tripping back to greet them with her silvery
laughter. But once she came back more sedately,
to say:

"There's a city a little way off."

"I 'spected that," returned Dorothy; "for the
fox-people warned us there was one on this road.
It's filled with stupid beasts of some sort, but we
mustn't be afraid of 'em 'cause they won't hurt
us."

"All right," said Button-Bright; but Polychrome didn't know whether it was all right or
not.

"It's a big city," she said, "and the road runs straight through it."

"Never mind," said the shaggy man; "as long as I carry the Love Magnet every living thing will love me, and you may be sure I shan't allow any of my friends to be harmed in any way."

This comforted them somewhat, and they moved on again. Pretty soon they came to a sign-post that read:

"HAF A MYLE TO DUNKITON."

"Oh," said the shaggy man, "if they're don-keys we've nothing to fear at all."

"They may kick," said Dorothy, doubtfully.

"Then we will cut some switches, and make them behave," he replied. At the first tree he cut himself a long, slender switch from one of the branches, and shorter switches for the others.

"Don't be afraid to order the beasts around," he said; "they're used to it."

Before long the road brought them to the gates of the city. There was a high wall all around, which had been whitewashed, and the gate just before our travelers was a mere opening in the wall, with no bars across it. No towers or steeples or domes showed above the enclosure, nor was any living thing to be seen as our friends drew near.

Suddenly, as they were about to boldly enter through the opening, there arose a harsh clamor of sound that swelled and echoed on every side, until they were nearly deafened by the racket and had to put their fingers to their ears to keep the noise out.

It was like the firing of many cannon, only there were no cannon-balls or other missiles to be seen; it was like the rolling of mighty thunder, only not a cloud was in the sky; it was like the roar of countless breakers on a rugged sea-shore, only there was no sea or other water anywhere about.

They hesitated to advance; but, as the noise did no harm, they entered through the white-washed wall and quickly discovered the cause of the turmoil. Inside were suspended many

sheets of tin or thin iron, and against these metal sheets a row of donkeys were pounding their heels with vicious kicks.

The shaggy man ran up to the nearest donkey and gave the beast a sharp blow with his switch.

"Stop that noise!" he shouted; and the donkey stopped kicking the metal sheet and turned its head to look with surprise at the shaggy man. He switched the next donkey, and made him stop, and then the next, so that gradually the rattling of heels ceased and the awful noise subsided. The donkeys stood in a group and eyed the strangers with fear and trembling.

"What do you mean by making such a racket?" asked the shaggy man, sternly.

"We were scaring away the foxes," said one of the donkeys, meekly. "Usually they run fast enough when they hear the noise, which makes them afraid."

"There are no foxes here," said the shaggy man.

"I beg to differ with you. There's one, anyhow," replied the donkey, sitting upright on its haunches and waving a hoof toward Button-Bright. "We saw him coming and thought the whole army of foxes was marching to attack us."

"Button-Bright isn't a fox," explained the shaggy man. "He's only wearing a fox head for a time, until he can get his own head back."

"Oh, I see," remarked the donkey, waving its left ear reflectively. "I'm sorry we made such a mistake, and had all our work and worry for nothing."

The other donkeys by this time were sitting up and examining the strangers with big, glassy eyes. They made a queer picture, indeed; for they wore wide, white collars around their necks and the collars had many scallops and points. The gentlemen-donkeys wore high pointed caps set between their great ears, and the lady-donkeys wore sunbonnets with holes cut in the top for the ears to stick through. But they had no other clothing except their hairy skins, although many wore gold and silver bangles on their front wrists and bands of different metals on their rear ankles. When they were kicking they had braced themselves with their front legs, but now they all stood or sat upright on their hind legs and used their front ones as arms. Having no fingers or hands the beasts were rather clumsy, as you may guess; but Dorothy was surprised to observe how many things they could do with their stiff, heavy hoofs.

Some of the donkeys were white, some were brown, or grey, or black, or spotted; but their hair was sleek and smooth and their broad collars and caps gave them a neat, if whimsical, appearance.

"This is a nice way to welcome visitors, I must say!" remarked the shaggy man, in a reproachful tone.

"Oh, we did not mean to be impolite," replied a grey donkey which had not spoken before. "But you were not expected, nor did you send in your visiting cards, as it is proper to do."

"There is some truth in that," admitted the shaggy man; "but, now you are informed that we are important and distinguished travelers, I trust you will accord us proper consideration."

These big words delighted the donkeys, and made them bow to the shaggy man with great respect. Said the grey one:

"You shall be taken before his great and glori-

ous Majesty King Kik-a-bray, who will greet you as becomes your exalted stations."

"That's right," answered Dorothy. "Take us to some one who knows something."

"Oh, we all know something, my child, or we shouldn't be donkeys," asserted the grey one, with dignity. "The word 'donkey' means 'clever,' you know."

"I didn't know it," she replied. "I thought it meant 'stupid'."

"Not at all, my child. If you will look in the Encyclopedia Donkaniara you will find I'm correct. But come; I will myself lead you before our splendid, exalted, and most intellectual ruler."

All donkeys love big words, so it is no wonder the grey one used so many of them.

The Shaggy Man's Transformation

THEY found the houses of the town all low and square and built of bricks, neatly white-washed inside and out. The houses were not set in rows, forming regular streets, but placed here and there in a haphazard manner which made it puzzling for a stranger to find his way.

"Stupid people must have streets and num-bered houses in their cities, to guide them where to go," observed the grey donkey, as he walked before the visitors on his hind legs, in an awk-ward but comical manner; "but clever donkeys know their way about without such absurd marks. Moreover, a mixed city is much prettier than one with straight streets."

Dorothy did not agree with this, but she said nothing to contradict it. Presently she saw a sign on a house that read: "Madam de Fayke, Hoof-ist," and she asked their conductor:

"What's a 'hoofist,' please?"

"One who reads your fortune in your hoofs," replied the grey donkey.

"Oh, I see," said the little girl. "You are quite civilized here."

"Dunkiton," he replied, "is the center of the world's highest civilization."

They came to a house where two youthful donkeys were whitewashing the wall, and Dorothy stopped a moment to watch them. They dipped the ends of their tails, which were much like paint-brushes, into a pail of whitewash, backed up against the house, and wagged their tails right and left until the whitewash was rubbed on the wall, after which they dipped these funny brushes in the pail again and repeated the performance.

"That must be fun," said Button-Bright.

"No; it's work," replied the old donkey; "but we make our youngsters do all the whitewashing, to keep them out of mischief."

"Don't they go to school?" asked Dorothy.

"All donkeys are born wise," was the reply, "so the only school we need is the school of experience. Books are only fit for those who know nothing, and so are obliged to learn things from other people."

"In other words, the more stupid one is, the more he thinks he knows," observed the shaggy man. The grey donkey paid no attention to this speech because he had just stopped before a house which had painted over the doorway a pair of hoofs, with a donkey tail between them and a rude crown and sceptre above.

"I'll see if his magnificent Majesty King Kik-a-bray is at home," said he. He lifted his head and called "Whee-haw! whee-haw! whee-haw!" three times, in a shocking voice, turning about and kicking with his heels against the panel of the door. For a time there was no reply; then the door opened far enough to permit a donkey's head to stick out and look at them.

It was a white head, with big, awful ears and round, solemn eyes.

"Have the foxes gone?" it asked, in a trembling voice.

"They haven't been here, most stupendous Majesty," replied the grey one. "The new arrivals prove to be travelers of distinction."

"Oh," said the King, in a relieved tone of voice. "Let them come in."

He opened the door wide, and the party marched into a big room, which, Dorothy thought, looked quite unlike a king's palace. There were mats of woven grasses on the floor and the place was clean and neat; but his Majesty had no other furniture at all—perhaps because he didn't need it. He squatted down in the center of the room and a little brown donkey ran and brought a big gold crown which it placed on the monarch's head, and a golden staff with a jeweled ball at the end of it, which the King held between his front hoofs as he sat upright.

"Now, then," said his Majesty, waving his long ears gently to and fro, "tell me why you are here, and what you expect me to do for you." He eyed Button-Bright rather sharply, as if afraid of the little boy's queer head, though it was the shaggy man who undertook to reply.

"Most noble and supreme ruler of Dunkiton," he said, trying not to laugh in the solemn King's face, "we are strangers traveling through your

dominions, and have entered your magnificent city because the road led through it, and there was no way to go around. All we desire is to pay our respects to your Majesty—the cleverest king in all the world, I'm sure—and then to continue on our way."

This polite speech pleased the King very much; indeed, it pleased him so much that it proved an unlucky speech for the shaggy man. Perhaps the Love Magnet helped to win his Majesty's affection as well as the flattery, but however this may be, the white donkey looked kindly upon the speaker and said:

"Only a donkey should be able to use such fine, big words, and you are too wise and admirable in all ways to be a mere man. Also I feel that I love you as well as I do my own favored people, so I will bestow upon you the greatest gift within my power—a donkey's head."

As he spoke he waved his jeweled staff. Although the shaggy man cried out and tried to leap backward and escape, it proved of no use. Suddenly his own head was gone and a donkey head appeared in its place—a brown, shaggy head so absurd and droll that Dorothy and Polly both broke into merry laughter, and even Button-Bright's fox face wore a smile.

"Dear me! dear me!" cried the shaggy man, feeling of his shaggy new head and his long ears. "What a misfortune—what a great misfortune! Give me back my own head, you stupid king—if you love me at all!"

"Don't you like it?" asked the King, surprised.

"Hee-haw! I hate it! Take it away—quick!" said the shaggy man.

"But I can't do that," was the reply. "My magic works only one way. I can *do* things, but I can't *un*do them. You'll have to find the Truth Pond, and bathe in its water, in order to get back your own head. But I advise you not to do that. This head is much more beautiful than the old one."

"That's a matter of taste," said Dorothy.

"Where is the Truth Pond?" asked the shaggy man, earnestly.

"Somewhere in the Land of Oz; but just the

KING KIK-A-BRAY WORKS MAGIC ON
THE SHAGGY MAN

exact location of it I can not tell," was the answer.

"Don't worry, Shaggy Man," said Dorothy, smiling because her friend wagged his new ears so comically. "If the Truth Pond is in Oz we'll be sure to find it when we get there."

"Oh! Are you going to the Land of Oz?" asked King Kik-a-bray.

"I don't know," she replied; "but we've been told we are nearer the Land of Oz than to Kansas, and if that's so, the quickest way for me to get home is to find Ozma."

"Haw-haw! Do you know the mighty Princess Ozma?" asked the King, his tone both surprised and eager.

" 'Course I do; she's my friend," said Dorothy.

"Then perhaps you'll do me a favor," continued the white donkey, much excited.

"What is it?" she asked.

"Perhaps you can get me an invitation to Princess Ozma's birthday celebration, which will be the grandest royal function ever held in Fairyland. I'd love to go."

"Hee-haw! You deserve punishment, rather than reward, for giving me this dreadful head," said the shaggy man, sorrowfully.

"I wish you wouldn't say 'hee-haw' so much," Polychrome begged him; "it makes cold chills run down my back."

"But I can't help it, my dear; my donkey head wants to bray continually," he replied. "Doesn't your fox head want to yelp every minute?" he asked Button-Bright.

"Don't know," said the boy, still staring at the shaggy man's ears. These seemed to interest him greatly, and the sight also made him forget his own fox head, which was a comfort.

"What do you think, Polly? Shall I promise the donkey king an invitation to Ozma's party?" asked Dorothy of the Rainbow's Daughter, who was flitting about the room like a sunbeam because she could never keep still.

"Do as you please, dear," answered Polychrome. "He might help to amuse the guests of the Princess."

"Then, if you will give us some supper and a place to sleep to-night, and let us get started on our journey early to-morrow morning," said Dorothy to the King, "I'll ask Ozma to invite you—if I happen to get to Oz."

"Good! Hee-haw! Excellent!" cried Kik-a-bray, much pleased. "You shall all have fine suppers and good beds. What food would you prefer, a bran mash or ripe oats in the shell?"

"Neither one," replied Dorothy, promptly.

"Perhaps plain hay, or some sweet juicy grass would suit you better," suggested Kik-a-bray, musingly.

"Is that all you have to eat?" asked the girl.

"What more do you desire?"

"Well, you see we're not donkeys," she explained, "and so we're used to other food. The foxes gave us a nice supper in Foxville."

"We'd like some dewdrops and mist-cakes," said Polychrome.

"I'd prefer apples and a ham sandwich," declared the shaggy man; "for although I've a donkey head I still have my own particular stomach."

"I want pie," said Button-Bright.

"I think some beefsteak and chocolate layer-cake would taste best," said Dorothy.

"Hee-haw! I declare!" exclaimed the King. "It

seems each one of you wants a different food. How queer all living creatures are, except donkeys!"

"And donkeys like you are queerest of all," laughed Polychrome.

"Well," decided the King, "I suppose my Magic Staff will produce the things you crave; if you are lacking in good taste it is not my fault."

With this he waved his staff with the jeweled ball, and before them instantly appeared a tea-table, set with linen and pretty dishes, and on the table were the very things each had wished for. Dorothy's beefsteak was smoking hot, and the shaggy man's apples were plump and rosy-cheeked. The King had not thought to provide chairs, so they all stood in their places around the table and ate with good appetite, being hungry. The Rainbow's Daughter found three tiny dewdrops on a crystal plate, and Button-Bright had a big slice of apple-pie, which he devoured eagerly.

Afterward the King called the brown donkey, which was his favorite servant, and bade it lead his guests to the vacant house where they were to pass the night. It had only one room and no furniture except beds of clean straw and a few mats of woven grasses; but our travelers were contented with these simple things because they realized it was the best the Donkey-King had to offer them. As soon as it was dark they lay down on the mats and slept comfortably until morning.

At daybreak there was a dreadful noise throughout the city. Every donkey in the place brayed. When he heard this the shaggy man woke up and called out "Hee-haw!" as loud as he could.

"Stop that!" said Button-Bright, in a cross voice. Both Dorothy and Polly looked at the shaggy man reproachfully.

"I couldn't help it, my dears," he said, as if ashamed of his bray; "but I'll try not to do it again."

Of course they forgave him, for as he still

had the Love Magnet in his pocket they were all obliged to love him as much as ever.

They did not see the King again, but Kik-a-bray remembered them; for a table appeared again in their room with the same food upon it as on the night before.

"Don't want pie for breakfus'," said Button-Bright.

"I'll give you some of my beefsteak," proposed Dorothy; "there's plenty for us all."

That suited the boy better, but the shaggy man said he was content with his apples and sandwiches, although he ended the meal by eating Button-Bright's pie. Polly liked her dewdrops and mist-cakes better than any other food, so they all enjoyed an excellent breakfast. Toto had the scraps left from the beefsteak, and he stood up nicely on his hind legs while Dorothy fed them to him.

Breakfast ended, they passed through the village to the side opposite that by which they had entered, the brown servant-donkey guiding them through the maze of scattered houses. There was the road again, leading far away into the unknown country beyond.

"King Kik-a-bray says you must not forget his invitation," said the brown donkey, as they passed through the opening in the wall.

"I shan't," promised Dorothy.

Perhaps no one ever beheld a more strangely assorted group than the one which now walked along the road, through pretty green fields and past groves of feathery pepper-trees and fragrant mimosa. Polychrome, her beautiful gauzy robes floating around her like a rainbow cloud, went first, dancing back and forth and darting now here to pluck a wild-flower or there to watch a beetle crawl across the path. Toto ran after her at times, barking joyously the while, only to be-

come sober again and trot along at Dorothy's heels. The little Kansas girl walked holding Button-Bright's hand clasped in her own, and the wee boy with his fox head covered by the sailor hat presented an odd appearance. Strangest of all, perhaps, was the shaggy man, with his shaggy donkey head, who shuffled along in the rear with his hands thrust deep in his big pockets.

None of the party was really unhappy. All

were straying in an unknown land and had suffered more or less annoyance and discomfort; but they realized they were having a fairy adventure in a fairy country, and were much interested in finding out what would happen next.

The Musicker

ABOUT the middle of the forenoon they began to go up a long hill. By-and-by this hill suddenly dropped down into a pretty valley, where the travelers saw, to their surprise, a small house standing by the road-side.

It was the first house they had seen, and they hastened into the valley to discover who lived there. No one was in sight as they approached, but when they began to get nearer the house they heard queer sounds coming from it. They could not make these out at first, but as they became louder our friends thought they heard a sort of music like that made by a wheezy hand-organ; the music fell upon their ears in this way:

Tiddle-widdle-iddle, oom pom-pom!
Oom, pom-pom! oom, pom-pom!
Tiddle-tiddle-tiddle, oom pom-pom!
Oom, pom-pom—pah!

"What is it, a band or a mouth-organ?" asked Dorothy.

"Don't know," said Button-Bright.

"Sounds to me like a played-out phonograph," said the shaggy man, lifting his enormous ears to listen.

"Oh, there just *couldn't* be a funnygraf in Fairyland!" cried Dorothy.

"It's rather pretty, isn't it?" asked Polychrome, trying to dance to the strains.

Tiddle-widdle-iddle, oom pom-pom,
Oom pom-pom; oom pom-pom!

came the music to their ears, more distinctly as they drew nearer the house. Presently they saw a little fat man sitting on a bench before the door. He wore a red, braided jacket that reached to his waist, a blue waistcoat, and white trousers with gold stripes down the sides. On his bald head was perched a little, round, red cap held in place by a rubber elastic underneath his chin. His face was round, his eyes a faded blue, and he wore white cotton gloves. The man leaned on

a stout gold-headed cane, bending forward on his seat to watch his visitors approach.

Singularly enough, the musical sounds they had heard seemed to come from the inside of the fat man himself; for he was playing no instrument nor was any to be seen near him.

They came up and stood in a row, staring at him, and he stared back while the queer sounds came from him as before:

> Tiddle-iddle-iddle, oom pom-pom,
>   Oom, pom-pom; oom pom-pom!
> Tiddle-widdle-iddle, oom pom-pom,
>   Oom, pom-pom—pah!

"Why, he's a reg'lar musicker!" said Button-Bright.

"What's a musicker?" asked Dorothy.

"Him!" said the boy.

Hearing this, the fat man sat up a little stiffer than before, as if he had received a compliment, and still came the sounds:

> *Tiddle-widdle-iddle, oom pom-pom,*
> *Oom pom-pom, oom——*

"Stop it!" cried the shaggy man, earnestly. "Stop that dreadful noise!"

The fat man looked at him sadly and began his reply. When he spoke the music changed and the words seemed to accompany the notes. He said—or rather sang:

> *It isn't a noise that you hear,*
> *But Music, harmonic and clear.*
> *My breath makes me play*
> *Like an organ, all day—*
> *That bass note is in my left ear.*

"How funny!" exclaimed Dorothy; "he says his breath makes the music."

"That's all nonsense," declared the shaggy man; but now the music began again, and they all listened carefully.

The Musicker

My lungs are full of reeds like those
In organs, therefore I suppose,
If I breathe in or out my nose,
  The reeds are bound to play.

So, as I breathe to live, you know,
I squeeze out music as I go;
I'm very sorry this is so——
  Forgive my piping, pray!

"Poor man," said Polychrome; "he can't help it. What a great misfortune it is!"

"Yes," replied the shaggy man; "we are only obliged to hear this music a short time, until we leave him and go away; but the poor fellow must listen to himself as long as he lives, and that is enough to drive him crazy. Don't you think so?"

"Don't know," said Button-Bright. Toto said "Bow-wow!" and the others laughed.

"Perhaps that's why he lives all alone," suggested Dorothy.

"Yes; if he had neighbors they might do him an injury," responded the shaggy man.

All this while the little fat musicker was breathing the notes:

Tiddle-tiddle-iddle, oom, pom-pom,

and they had to speak loud in order to hear themselves. The shaggy man said:

"Who are you, sir?"

The reply came in the shape of this sing-song:

I'm Allegro da Capo, a very famous man;
Just find another, high or low, to match me if
*   you can.*
*   Some people try, but can't, to play*
*   And have to practice every day;*
But I've been musical always, since first my life
*   began.*

"Why, I b'lieve he's proud of it," exclaimed Dorothy; "and seems to me I've heard worse music than he makes."

"Where?" asked Button-Bright.

"I've forgotten, just now. But Mr. Da Capo is

certainly a strange person—isn't he?—and p'r'aps he's the only one of his kind in all the world."

This praise seemed to please the little fat musicker, for he swelled out his chest, looked important and sang as follows:

> *I wear no band around me,*
> *   And yet I am a band!*
> *I do not strain to make my strains*
> *   But, on the other hand,*
> *My toot is always destitute*
> *   Of flats or other errors;*
> *To see sharp and be natural are*
> *   For me but minor terrors.*

"I don't quite understand that," said Polychrome, with a puzzled look; "but perhaps it's because I'm accustomed only to the music of the spheres."

"What's that?" asked Button-Bright.

"Oh, Polly means the atmosphere and hemi-sphere, I s'pose," explained Dorothy.

"Oh," said Button-Bright.

"Bow-wow!" said Toto.

But the musicker was still breathing his constant

Oom, pom-pom; oom, pom-pom—

and it seemed to jar on the shaggy man's nerves.

"Stop it, can't you?" he cried, angrily; "or breathe in a whisper; or put a clothes-pin on your nose. Do something, anyhow!"

But the fat one, with a sad look, sang this answer:

> *Music hath charms, and it may*
> *Soothe even the savage, they say;*
> *So if savage you feel*
> *Just list to my reel,*
> *For sooth to say that's the real way.*

The shaggy man had to laugh at this, and when he laughed he stretched his donkey mouth wide open. Said Dorothy:

"I don't know how good his poetry is, but it seems to fit the notes, so that's all that can be 'xpected."

"I like it," said Button-Bright, who was staring hard at the musicker, his little legs spread wide apart. To the surprise of his companions, the boy asked this long question:

"If I swallowed a mouth-organ, what would I be?"

"An organette," said the shaggy man. "But come, my dears; I think the best thing we can do is to continue on our journey before Button-Bright swallows anything. We must try to find that Land of Oz, you know."

Hearing this speech the musicker sang, quickly:

> *If you go to the Land of Oz*
> *Please take me along, because*
> *On Ozma's birthday*
> *I'm anxious to play*
> *The loveliest song ever was.*

"No, thank you," said Dorothy; "we prefer to travel alone. But if I see Ozma I'll tell her you want to come to her birthday party."

"Let's be going," urged the shaggy man, anxiously.

Polly was already dancing along the road, far in advance, and the others turned to follow her. Toto did not like the fat musicker and made a grab for his chubby leg. Dorothy quickly caught up the growling little dog and hurried after her companions, who were walking faster than usual in order to get out of hearing. They had to climb a hill, and until they got to the top they could not escape the musicker's monotonous piping:

Oom, pom-pom; oom, pom-pom;
Tiddle-iddle-widdle, oom, pom-pom;
Oom, pom-pom—pah!

As they passed the brow of the hill, however, and descended on the other side, the sounds gradually died away, whereat they all felt much relieved.

"I'm glad I don't have to live with the organman; aren't you, Polly?" said Dorothy.

"Yes, indeed," answered the Rainbow's Daughter.

"He's nice," declared Button-Bright, soberly.

"I hope your Princess Ozma won't invite him to her birthday celebration," remarked the shaggy man; "for the fellow's music would drive her guests all crazy. You've given me an idea,

Button-Bright; I believe the musicker must have swallowed an accordeon in his youth."

"What's 'cordeon?" asked the boy.

"It's a kind of pleating," explained Dorothy, putting down the dog.

"Bow-wow!" said Toto, and ran away at a mad gallop to chase a bumble-bee.

Facing the Scoodlers

THE country wasn't so pretty now. Before the travelers appeared a rocky plain covered with hills on which grew nothing green. They were nearing some low mountains, too, and the road, which before had been smooth and pleasant to walk upon, grew rough and uneven.

Button-Bright's little feet stumbled more than once, and Polychrome ceased her dancing because the walking was now so difficult that she had no trouble to keep warm.

It had become afternoon, yet there wasn't a thing for their luncheon except two apples which the shaggy man had taken from the breakfast table. He divided these into four pieces and gave a portion to each of his companions. Dorothy and Button-Bright were glad to get theirs;

but Polly was satisfied with a small bite, and Toto did not like apples.

"Do you know," asked the Rainbow's Daughter, "if this is the right road to the Emerald City?"

"No, I don't," replied Dorothy; "but it's the only road in this part of the country, so we may as well go to the end of it."

"It looks now as if it might end pretty soon," remarked the shaggy man; "and what shall we do if it does?"

"Don't know," said Button-Bright.

"If I had my Magic Belt," replied Dorothy, thoughtfully, "it could do us a lot of good just now."

"What is your Magic Belt?" asked Polly-chrome.

"It's a thing I captured from the Nome King one day, and it can do 'most any wonderful thing. But I left it with Ozma, you know; 'cause magic won't work in Kansas, but only in fairy countries."

"Is this a fairy country?" asked Button-Bright.

"I should think you'd know," said the little girl, gravely. "If it wasn't a fairy country you couldn't have a fox head and the shaggy man couldn't have a donkey head, and the Rainbow's Daughter would be invis'ble."

"What's that?" asked the boy.

"You don't seem to know anything, Button-
Bright. Invis'ble is a thing you can't see."

"Then Toto's invis'ble," declared the boy, and
Dorothy found he was right. Toto had disappeared from view, but they could hear him barking furiously among the heaps of grey rock
ahead of them.

They moved forward a little faster to see
what the dog was barking at, and found perched
upon a point of rock by the roadside a curious
creature. It had the form of a man, middle-sized
and rather slender and graceful; but as it sat
silent and motionless upon the peak they could
see that its face was black as ink, and it wore a
black cloth costume made like a union suit and
fitting tight to its skin. Its hands were black,

too, and its toes curled down, like a bird's. The creature was black all over except its hair, which was fine, and yellow, banged in front across the black forehead and cut close at the sides. The eyes, which were fixed steadily upon the barking dog, were small and sparkling and looked like the eyes of a weasel.

"What in the world do you s'pose that is?" asked Dorothy in a hushed voice, as the little group of travelers stood watching the strange creature.

"Don't know," said Button-Bright.

The thing gave a jump and turned half around, sitting in the same place but with the other side of its body facing them. Instead of being black, it was now pure white, with a face like that of a clown in a circus and hair of a brilliant purple. The creature could bend either way, and its white toes now curled the same way the black ones on the other side had done.

"It has a face both front and back," whispered Dorothy, wonderingly; "only there's no back at all, but two fronts."

Having made the turn, the being sat motionless as before, while Toto barked louder at the white man than he had done at the black one.

"Once," said the shaggy man, "I had a jumping-jack like that, with two faces."

"Was it alive?" asked Button-Bright.

"No," replied the shaggy man; "it worked on strings, and was made of wood."

"Wonder if this works with strings," said Dorothy; but Polychrome cried "Look!" for another creature just like the first had suddenly appeared sitting on another rock, its black side toward them. The two twisted their heads around and showed a black face on the white side of one and a white face on the black side of the other.

"How curious," said Polychrome; "and how loose their heads seem to be! Are they friendly to us, do you think?"

"Can't tell, Polly," replied Dorothy. "Let's ask 'em."

The creatures flopped first one way and then the other, showing black or white by turns; and now another joined them, appearing on another rock. Our friends had come to a little hollow in the hills, and the place where they now stood was surrounded by jagged peaks of rock, except where the road ran through.

"Now there are four of them," said the shaggy man.

"Five," declared Polychrome.

"Six," said Dorothy.

"Lots of 'em!" cried Button-Bright; and so there were—quite a row of the two-sided black and white creatures sitting on the rocks all around.

Toto stopped barking and ran between Dorothy's feet, where he crouched down as if afraid. The creatures did not look pleasant or friendly, to be sure, and the shaggy man's donkey face became solemn, indeed.

"Ask 'em who they are, and what they want," whispered Dorothy; so the shaggy man called out in a loud voice:

"Who are you?"

"Scoodlers!" they yelled in chorus, their voices sharp and shrill.

"What do you want?" called the shaggy man.

"You!" they yelled, pointing their thin fingers

"YOU!" THEY YELLED

at the group; and they all flopped around, so they were white, and then all flopped back again, so they were black.

"But what do you want us for?" asked the shaggy man, uneasily.

"Soup!" they all shouted, as if with one voice.

"Goodness me!" said Dorothy, trembling a little; "the Scoodlers must be reg'lar cannibals."

"Don't want to be soup," protested Button-Bright, beginning to cry.

"Hush, dear," said the little girl, trying to comfort him; "we don't any of us want to be soup. But don't worry; the shaggy man will take care of us."

"Will he?" asked Polychrome, who did not like the Scoodlers at all, and kept close to Dorothy.

"I'll try," promised the shaggy man; but he looked worried.

Happening just then to feel the Love Magnet in his pocket, he said to the creatures, with more confidence:

"Don't you love me?"

"Yes!" they shouted, all together.

"Then you mustn't harm me, or my friends," said the shaggy man, firmly.

"We love you in soup!" they yelled, and in a flash turned their white sides to the front.

"How dreadful!" said Dorothy. "This is a

time, Shaggy Man, when you get loved too much."

"Don't want to be soup!" wailed Button-Bright again; and Toto began to whine dismally, as if he didn't want to be soup, either.

"The only thing to do," said the shaggy man to his friends, in a low tone, "is to get out of this pocket in the rocks as soon as we can, and leave the Scoodlers behind us. Follow me, my dears, and don't pay any attention to what they do or say."

With this he began to march along the road to the opening in the rocks ahead, and the others kept close behind him. But the Scoodlers closed up in front, as if to bar their way, and so the shaggy man stooped down and picked up a loose

stone, which he threw at the creatures to scare them from the path.

At this the Scoodlers raised a howl. Two of them picked their heads from their shoulders and hurled them at the shaggy man with such force that he fell over in a heap, greatly astonished. The two now ran forward with swift leaps, caught up their heads, and put them on again, after which they sprang back to their positions on the rocks.

Escaping the Soup-Kettle

THE shaggy man got up and felt of himself to see if he was hurt; but he was not. One of the heads had struck his breast and the other his left shoulder; yet though they had knocked him down, the heads were not hard enough to bruise him.

"Come on," he said, firmly; "we've got to get out of here some way," and forward he started again.

The Scoodlers began yelling and throwing their heads in great numbers at our frightened friends. The shaggy man was knocked over again, and so was Button-Bright, who kicked his heels against the ground and howled as loud as he could, although he was not hurt a bit. One head struck Toto, who first yelped and then grabbed the head by an ear and started running away with it.

The Scoodlers who had thrown their heads began to scramble down and run to pick them up, with wonderful quickness; but the one whose head Toto had stolen found it hard to get it back again. The head couldn't see the body with either pair of its eyes, because the dog was in the way, so the headless Scoodler stumbled around over the rocks and tripped on them more than once in its effort to regain its top. Toto was trying to get outside the rocks and roll the head down the hill; but some of the other Scoodlers came to the rescue of their unfortunate comrade and pelted the dog with their own heads until he was obliged to drop his burden and hurry back to Dorothy.

The little girl and the Rainbow's Daughter had both escaped the shower of heads, but they saw now that it would be useless to try to run away from the dreadful Scoodlers.

"We may as well submit," declared the shaggy man, in a rueful voice, as he got upon his feet again. He turned toward their foes and asked:

"What do you want us to do?"

"Come!" they cried, in a triumphant chorus, and at once sprang from the rocks and surrounded their captives on all sides. One funny thing about the Scoodlers was they could walk

in either direction, coming or going, without turning around; because they had two faces and, as Dorothy said, "two front sides," and their feet were shaped like the letter T upside down (⊥). They moved with great rapidity and there was something about their glittering eyes and contrasting colors and removable heads that inspired the poor prisoners with horror, and made them long to escape.

But the creatures led their captives away from the rocks and the road, down the hill by a side path until they came before a low mountain of rock that looked like a huge bowl turned upside down. At the edge of this mountain was a deep gulf—so deep that when you looked into it there was nothing but blackness below. Across the gulf was a narrow bridge of rock, and at the other end of the bridge was an arched opening that led into the mountain.

Over this bridge the Scoodlers led their prisoners, through the opening into the mountain, which they found to be an immense hollow dome lighted by several holes in the roof. All around the circular space were built rock houses, set close together, each with a door in the front wall. None of these houses was more than six feet wide, but the Scoodlers were thin people sidewise and did not need much room. So vast was the dome that there was a large space in the middle of the cave, in front of all these houses, where the creatures might congregate as in a great hall.

It made Dorothy shudder to see a huge iron kettle suspended by a stout chain in the middle of the place, and underneath the kettle a great heap of kindling wood and shavings, ready to light.

"What's that?" asked the shaggy man, drawing back as they approached this place, so that they were forced to push him forward.

"The Soup Kettle!" yelled the Scoodlers; and then they shouted in the next breath:

"We're hungry!"

Button-Bright, holding Dorothy's hand in one

chubby fist and Polly's hand in the other, was so affected by this shout that he began to cry again, repeating the protest:

"Don't want to be soup, I don't!"

"Never mind," said the shaggy man, consolingly; "I ought to make enough soup to feed them all, I'm so big; so I'll ask them to put me in the kettle first."

"All right," said Button-Bright, more cheerfully.

But the Scoodlers were not ready to make soup yet. They led the captives into a house at the farthest side of the cave—a house somewhat wider than the others.

"Who lives here?" asked the Rainbow's Daughter. The Scoodlers nearest her replied:

"The Queen."

It made Dorothy hopeful to learn that a woman ruled over these fierce creatures, but a moment later they were ushered by two or three of the escort into a gloomy, bare room—and her hope died away.

For the Queen of the Scoodlers proved to be much more dreadful in appearance than any of her people. One side of her was fiery red, with jet-black hair and green eyes and the other side of her was bright yellow, with crimson hair and black eyes. She wore a short skirt of red and yellow and her hair, instead of being banged,

was a tangle of short curls upon which rested a circular crown of silver—much dented and twisted because the Queen had thrown her head at so many things so many times. Her form was lean and bony and both her faces were deeply wrinkled.

"What have we here?" asked the Queen, sharply, as our friends were made to stand before her.

"Soup!" cried the guard of Scoodlers, speaking together.

"We're not!" said Dorothy, indignantly; "we're nothing of the sort."

"Ah, but you will be soon," retorted the Queen, a grim smile making her look more dreadful than before.

"Pardon me, most beautiful vision," said the

shaggy man, bowing before the queen politely. "I must request your Serene Highness to let us go our way without being made into soup. For I own the Love Magnet, and whoever meets me must love me and all my friends."

"True," replied the Queen. "We love you very much; so much that we intend to eat your broth with real pleasure. But tell me, do you think I am so beautiful?"

"You won't be at all beautiful if you eat me," he said, shaking his head sadly. "Handsome is as handsome does, you know."

The Queen turned to Button-Bright.

"Do *you* think I'm beautiful?" she asked.

"No," said the boy; "you're ugly."

"*I* think you're a fright," said Dorothy.

"If you could see yourself you'd be terribly scared," added Polly.

The Queen scowled at them and flopped from her red side to her yellow side.

"Take them away," she commanded the guard, "and at six o'clock run them through the meat chopper and start the soup kettle boiling. And put plenty of salt in the broth this time, or I'll punish the cooks severely."

"Any onions, your Majesty?" asked one of the guard.

"Plenty of onions and garlic and a dash of red pepper. Now, go!"

The Scoodlers led the captives away and shut them up in one of the houses, leaving only a single Scoodler to keep guard.

The place was a sort of store-house; containing bags of potatoes and baskets of carrots, onions, and turnips.

"These," said their guard, pointing to the vegetables, "we use to flavor our soups with."

The prisoners were rather disheartened by this time, for they saw no way to escape and did not know how soon it would be six o'clock and time for the meat chopper to begin work. But the shaggy man was brave and did not intend to submit to such a horrid fate without a struggle.

"I'm going to fight for our lives," he whispered to the children, "for if I fail we will be no worse

off than before, and to sit here quietly until we are made into soup would be foolish and cowardly."

The Scoodler on guard stood near the doorway, turning first his white side toward them and then his black side, as if he wanted to show to all of his greedy four eyes the sight of so many fat prisoners. The captives sat in a sorrowful group at the other end of the room—except Polychrome, who danced back and forth in the little place to keep herself warm, for she felt the chill of the cave. Whenever she approached the shaggy man he would whisper something in her ear, and Polly would nod her pretty head as if she understood.

The shaggy man told Dorothy and Button-Bright to stand before him while he emptied the potatoes out of one of the sacks. When this had been secretly done, little Polychrome, dancing near to the guard, suddenly reached out her hand and slapped his face, the next instant whirling away from him quickly to rejoin her friends.

The angry Scoodler at once picked off his head and hurled it at the Rainbow's Daughter; but the shaggy man was expecting that, and caught the head very neatly, putting it in the sack, which he tied at the mouth. The body of the guard, not having the eyes of its head to

THE SHAGGY MAN CAUGHT THE HEADS AND
TOSSED THEM INTO THE GULF BELOW

guide it, ran here and there in an aimless manner, and the shaggy man easily dodged it and opened the door. Fortunately there was no one in the big cave at that moment, so he told Dorothy and Polly to run as fast as they could for the entrance, and out across the narrow bridge.

"I'll carry Button-Bright," he said, for he knew the little boy's legs were too short to run fast.

Dorothy picked up Toto, and then seized Polly's hand and ran swiftly toward the entrance to the cave. The shaggy man perched Button-Bright on his shoulders and ran after them. They moved so quickly and their escape was so wholly unexpected that they had almost reached the bridge when one of the Scoodlers looked out of his house and saw them.

The creature raised a shrill cry that brought all its fellows bounding out of the numerous doors, and at once they started in chase. Dorothy and Polly had reached the bridge and crossed it when the Scoodlers began throwing their heads. One of the queer missiles struck the shaggy man on his back and nearly knocked him over; but he was at the mouth of the cave now, so he set down Button-Bright and told the boy to run across the bridge to Dorothy.

Then the shaggy man turned around and faced his enemies, standing just outside the opening, and as fast as they threw their heads at him he caught them and tossed them into the black gulf below. The headless bodies of the foremost Scoodlers kept the others from running close up, but they also threw their heads in an effort to stop the escaping prisoners. The shaggy man caught them all and sent them whirling down into the black gulf. Among them he no-

ticed the crimson and yellow head of the Queen, and this he tossed after the others with right good will.

Presently every Scoodler of the lot had thrown its head, and every head was down in the deep gulf, and now the helpless bodies of the creatures were mixed together in the cave and wriggling around in a vain attempt to discover what had become of their heads. The shaggy man laughed and walked across the bridge to rejoin his companions.

"It's lucky I learned to play base-ball when I was young," he remarked, "for I caught all those heads easily, and never missed one. But come along, little ones; the Scoodlers will never bother us or anyone else any more."

Button-Bright was still frightened and kept insisting, "I don't want to be soup!" for the victory had been gained so suddenly that the boy could not realize they were free and safe. But the shaggy man assured him that all danger of their being made into soup was now past, as the Scoodlers would be unable to eat soup for some time to come.

So now, anxious to get away from the horrid gloomy cave as soon as possible, they hastened up the hillside and regained the road just beyond the place where they had first met the Scoodlers; and you may be sure they were glad to find their feet on the old familiar path again.

Johnny Dooit Does It

"IT'S getting awful rough walking," said Dorothy, as they trudged along. Button-Bright gave a deep sigh and said he was hungry. Indeed, all were hungry, and thirsty, too; for they had eaten nothing but the apples since breakfast; so their steps lagged and they grew silent and weary. At last they slowly passed over the crest of a barren hill and saw before them a line of green trees with a strip of grass at their feet. An agreeable fragrance was wafted toward them.

Our travelers, hot and tired, ran forward on beholding this refreshing sight and were not long in coming to the trees. Here they found a spring of pure bubbling water, around which the grass was full of wild strawberry plants, their pretty red berries ripe and ready to eat. Some of the trees bore yellow oranges and some russet pears, so the hungry adventurers suddenly found themselves provided with plenty to eat and to drink.

They lost no time in picking the biggest strawberries and ripest oranges and soon had feasted to their hearts' content. Walking beyond the line of trees they saw before them a fearful, dismal desert, everywhere grey sand. At the edge of this awful waste was a large white sign with black letters neatly painted upon it; and the letters made these words:

ALL PERSONS ARE WARNED NOT TO VENTURE UPON THIS DESERT

For the Deadly Sands will Turn Any Living Flesh to Dust in an Instant. Beyond This Barrier is the

LAND OF OZ

But no one can Reach that Beautiful Country because of these Destroying Sands

---

"Oh," said Dorothy, when the shaggy man had read this sign aloud; "I've seen this desert before, and it's true no one can live who tries to walk upon the sands."

"Then we mustn't try it," answered the shaggy

man, thoughtfully. "But as we can't go ahead and there's no use going back, what shall we do next?"

"Don't know," said Button-Bright.

"I'm sure I don't know, either," added Dorothy, despondently.

"I wish father would come for me," sighed the pretty Rainbow's Daughter, "I would take you all to live upon the rainbow, where you could dance along its rays from morning till night, without a care or worry of any sort. But I suppose father's too busy just now to search the world for me."

"Don't want to dance," said Button-Bright, sitting down wearily upon the soft grass.

"It's very good of you, Polly," said Dorothy; "but there are other things that would suit me

better than dancing on rainbows. I'm 'fraid
they'd be kind of soft an' squnshy under foot,
anyhow, although they're so pretty to look at."

This didn't help to solve the problem, and
they all fell silent and looked at one another
questioningly.

"Really, I don't know what to do," muttered
the shaggy man, gazing hard at Toto; and the
little dog wagged his tail and said "Bow-wow!"
just as if he could not tell, either, what to do.
Button-Bright got a stick and began to dig in
the earth, and the others watched him for a
while in deep thought. Finally the shaggy man
said:

"It's nearly evening, now; so we may as well
sleep in this pretty place and get rested; perhaps
by morning we can decide what is best to be
done."

There was little chance to make beds for the
children, but the leaves of the trees grew thickly
and would serve to keep off the night dews, so
the shaggy man piled soft grasses in the thickest
shade and when it was dark they lay down and
slept peacefully until morning.

Long after the others were asleep, however,
the shaggy man sat in the starlight by the spring,
gazing thoughtfully into its bubbling waters.
Suddenly he smiled and nodded to himself as

if he had found a good thought, after which he, too, laid himself down under a tree and was soon lost in slumber.

In the bright morning sunshine, as they ate of the strawberries and sweet juicy pears, Dorothy said:

"Polly, can you do any magic?"

"No, dear," answered Polychrome, shaking her dainty head.

"You ought to know *some* magic, being the Rainbow's Daughter," continued Dorothy, earnestly.

"But we who live on the rainbow among the fleecy clouds have no use for magic," replied Polychrome.

"What I'd like," said Dorothy, "is to find some way to cross the desert to the Land of Oz and its Emerald City. I've crossed it already, you know, more than once. First a cyclone carried my house over, and some Silver Shoes brought me back again—in half a second. Then Ozma took me over on her Magic Carpet, and the Nome King's Magic Belt took me home that time. You see it was magic that did it every time 'cept the first, and we can't 'spect a cyclone to happen along and take us to the Emerald City now."

"No, indeed," returned Polly, with a shudder; "I hate cyclones, anyway."

"That's why I wanted to find out if you could do any magic," said the little Kansas girl. "I'm sure I can't; and I'm sure Button-Bright can't; and the only magic the shaggy man has is the Love Magnet, which won't help us much."

"Don't be too sure of that, my dear," spoke the shaggy man, a smile on his donkey face. "I may not be able to do magic myself, but I can call to us a powerful friend who loves me because I own the Love Magnet, and this friend surely will be able to help us."

"Who is your friend?" asked Dorothy.

"Johnny Dooit."

"What can Johnny do?"

"Anything," answered the shaggy man, with confidence.

"Ask him to come," she exclaimed, eagerly.

The shaggy man took the Love Magnet from his pocket and unwrapped the paper that surrounded it. Holding the charm in the palm of his hand he looked at it steadily and said these words:

> "Dear Johnny Dooit, come to me.
> I need you bad as bad can be."

"Well, here I am," said a cheery little voice; "but you shouldn't say you need me bad, 'cause I'm always, *always* good."

At this they quickly whirled around to find a funny little man sitting on a big copper chest, puffing smoke from a long pipe. His hair was grey, his whiskers were grey; and these whiskers were so long that he had wound the ends of them around his waist and tied them in a hard knot underneath the leather apron that reached from his chin nearly to his feet, and which was

soiled and scratched as if it had been used a long time. His nose was broad, and stuck up a little; but his eyes were twinkling and merry. The little man's hands and arms were as hard and tough as the leather in his apron, and Dorothy thought Johnny Dooit looked as if he had done a lot of hard work in his lifetime.

"Good morning, Johnny," said the shaggy

man. "Thank you for coming to me so quickly."

"I never waste time," said the newcomer, promptly. "But what's happened to you? Where did you get that donkey head? Really, I wouldn't have known you at all, Shaggy Man, if I hadn't looked at your feet."

The shaggy man introduced Johnny Dooit to Dorothy and Toto and Button-Bright and the Rainbow's Daughter, and told him the story of their adventures, adding that they were anxious now to reach the Emerald City in the Land of Oz, where Dorothy had friends who would take care of them and send them safe home again.

"But," said he, "we find that we can't cross this desert, which turns all living flesh that touches it into dust; so I have asked you to come and help us."

Johnny Dooit puffed his pipe and looked carefully at the dreadful desert in front of them—stretching so far away they could not see its end.

"You must ride," he said, briskly.

"What in?" asked the shaggy man.

"In a sand-boat, which has runners like a sled and sails like a ship. The wind will blow you swiftly across the desert and the sand cannot touch your flesh to turn it into dust."

"Good!" cried Dorothy, clapping her hands delightedly. "That was the way the Magic Carpet took us across. We didn't have to touch the horrid sand at all."

"But where is the sand-boat?" asked the shaggy man, looking all around him.

"I'll make you one," said Johnny Dooit.

As he spoke he knocked the ashes from his pipe and put it in his pocket. Then he unlocked the copper chest and lifted the lid, and Dorothy saw it was full of shining tools of all sorts and shapes.

Johnny Dooit moved quickly now—so quickly that they were astonished at the work he was able to accomplish. He had in his chest a tool for everything he wanted to do, and these must have been magic tools because they did their work so fast and so well.

The man hummed a little song as he worked, and Dorothy tried to listen to it. She thought the words were something like these:

> The only way to do a thing
> Is do it when you can,
> And do it cheerfully, and sing
> And work and think and plan.
> The only real unhappy one
> Is he who dares to shirk;
> The only really happy one
> Is he who cares to work.

Whatever Johnny Dooit was singing he was certainly doing things, and they all stood by and watched him in amazement.

He seized an axe and in a couple of chops felled a tree. Next he took a saw and in a few minutes sawed the tree-trunk into broad long boards. He then nailed the boards together into the shape of a boat, about twelve feet long and four feet wide. He cut from another tree a long, slender pole which, when trimmed of its branches and fastened upright in the center of the boat, served as a mast. From the chest he drew a coil of rope and a big bundle of canvas, and with these—still humming his song—he rigged up a sail, arranging it so it could be raised or lowered upon the mast.

125

Dorothy fairly gasped with wonder to see the thing grow so speedily before her eyes, and both Button-Bright and Polly looked on with the same absorbed interest.

"It ought to be painted," said Johnny Dooit, tossing his tools back into the chest, "for that would make it look prettier. But 'though I can paint it for you in three seconds it would take an hour to dry, and that's a waste of time."

"We don't care how it looks," said the shaggy man, "if only it will take us across the desert."

"It will do that," declared Johnny Dooit. "All you need worry about is tipping over. Did you ever sail a ship?"

"I've seen one sailed," said the shaggy man.

"Good. Sail this boat the way you've seen a ship sailed, and you'll be across the sands before you know it."

With this he slammed down the lid of the chest, and the noise made them all wink. While they were winking the workman disappeared, tools and all.

The Deadly Desert Crossed

"OH, that's too bad!" cried Dorothy; "I wanted to thank Johnny Dooit for all his kindness to us."

"He hasn't time to listen to thanks," replied the shaggy man; "but I'm sure he knows we are grateful. I suppose he is already at work in some other part of the world."

They now looked more carefully at the sand-boat, and saw that the bottom was modeled with two sharp runners which would glide through the sand. The front of the sand-boat was pointed like the bow of a ship, and there was a rudder at the stern to steer by.

It had been built just at the edge of the desert, so that all its length lay upon the grey sand except the after part, which still rested on the strip of grass.

"Get in, my dears," said the shaggy man; "I'm sure I can manage this boat as well as any sailor. All you need do is sit still in your places."

Dorothy got in, Toto in her arms, and sat on the bottom of the boat just in front of the mast. Button-Bright sat in front of Dorothy, while Polly leaned over the bow. The shaggy man knelt behind the mast. When all were ready he

raised the sail half way. The wind caught it. At once the sand-boat started forward—slowly at first, then with added speed. The shaggy man pulled the sail way up, and they flew so fast over the Deadly Desert that every one held fast to the sides of the boat and scarcely dared to breathe.

The sand lay in billows, and was in places very uneven, so that the boat rocked dangerously from side to side; but it never quite tipped over, and the speed was so great that the shaggy man himself became frightened and began to wonder how he could make the ship go slower.

"If we're spilled in this sand, in the middle of the desert," Dorothy thought to herself, "we'll be nothing but dust in a few minutes, and that will be the end of us."

But they were not spilled, and by-and-by Polychrome, who was clinging to the bow and looking straight ahead, saw a dark line before them and wondered what it was. It grew plainer every second, until she discovered it to be a row of jagged rocks at the end of the desert, while high above these rocks she could see a tableland of green grass and beautiful trees.

"Look out!" she screamed to the shaggy man. "Go slowly, or we shall smash into the rocks."

He heard her, and tried to pull down the sail; but the wind would not let go of the broad canvas and the ropes had become tangled.

Nearer and nearer they drew to the great rocks, and the shaggy man was in despair because he could do nothing to stop the wild rush of the sand-boat.

They reached the edge of the desert and bumped squarely into the rocks. There was a crash as Dorothy, Button-Bright, Toto and Polly flew up in the air in a curve like a skyrocket's,

"LOOK OUT!" SCREAMED POLYCHROME

one after another landing high upon the grass,
where they rolled and tumbled for a time before
they could stop themselves.

The shaggy man flew after them, head first,
and lighted in a heap beside Toto, who, being
much excited at the time, seized one of the donkey ears between his teeth and shook and worried it as hard as he could, growling angrily.
The shaggy man made the little dog let go, and
sat up to look around him.

Dorothy was feeling one of her front teeth,
which was loosened by knocking against her
knee as she fell. Polly was looking sorrowfully
at a rent in her pretty gauze gown, and Button-
Bright's fox head had stuck fast in a gopher hole
and he was wiggling his little fat legs frantically
in an effort to get free.

Otherwise they were unhurt by the adventure;
so the shaggy man stood up and pulled Button-
Bright out of the hole and went to the edge of
the desert to look at the sand-boat. It was a mere
mass of splinters now, crushed out of shape
against the rocks. The wind had torn away the
sail and carried it to the top of a tall tree, where
the fragments of it fluttered like a white flag.

"Well," he said, cheerfully, "we're here; but
where the here is I don't know."

"It must be some part of the Land of Oz,"
observed Dorothy, coming to his side.

"Must it?"

" 'Course it must. We're across the desert, aren't we? And somewhere in the middle of Oz is the Emerald City."

"To be sure," said the shaggy man, nodding. "Let's go there."

"But I don't see any people about, to show us the way," she continued.

"Let's hunt for them," he suggested. "There must be people somewhere; but perhaps they did not expect us, and so are not at hand to give us a welcome."

The Truth Pond

THEY now made a more careful examination of the country around them. All was fresh and beautiful after the sultriness of the desert, and the sunshine and sweet, crisp air were delightful to the wanderers. Little mounds of yellowish green were away at the right, while on the left waved a group of tall leafy trees bearing yellow blossoms that looked like tassels and pompoms. Among the grasses carpeting the ground were pretty buttercups and cowslips and marigolds. After looking at these a moment Dorothy said reflectively:

"We must be in the Country of the Winkies, for the color of that country is yellow, and you will notice that 'most everything here is yellow that has any color at all."

"But I thought this was the Land of Oz," replied the shaggy man, as if greatly disappointed.

"So it is," she declared; "but there are four parts to the Land of Oz. The North Country is purple, and it's the Country of the Gillikins. The East Country is blue, and that's the Country of the Munchkins. Down at the South is the red Country of the Quadlings, and here, in the West, the yellow Country of the Winkies. This is the part that is ruled by the Tin Woodman, you know."

"Who's he?" asked Button-Bright.

"Why, he's the tin man I told you about. His name is Nick Chopper, and he has a lovely heart given him by the wonderful Wizard."

"Where does *he* live?" asked the boy.

"The Wizard? Oh, he lives in the Emerald City, which is just in the middle of Oz, where the corners of the four countries meet."

"Oh," said Button-Bright, puzzled by this explanation.

"We must be some distance from the Emerald City," remarked the shaggy man.

"That's true," she replied; "so we'd better start on and see if we can find any of the Winkies. They're nice people," she continued, as the little party began walking toward the group of trees, "and I came here once with my friends the Scarecrow, and the Tin Woodman,

and the Cowardly Lion, to fight a wicked witch who had made all the Winkies her slaves."

"Did you conquer her?" asked Polly.

"Why, I melted her with a bucket of water, and that was the end of her," replied Dorothy. "After that the people were free, you know, and they made Nick Chopper—that's the Tin Woodman—their Emp'ror."

"What's that?" asked Button-Bright.

"Emp'ror? Oh, it's something like an alderman, I guess."

"Oh," said the boy.

"But I thought Princess Ozma ruled Oz," said the shaggy man.

"So she does; she rules the Emerald City and all the four countries of Oz; but each country has another little ruler, not so big as Ozma. It's like the officers of an army, you see; the little rulers are all captains, and Ozma's the general."

By this time they had reached the trees, which stood in a perfect circle and just far enough apart so that their thick branches touched—or "shook hands," as Button-Bright remarked. Under the shade of the trees they found, in the center of the circle, a crystal pool, its water as still as glass. It must have been deep, too, for when Polychrome bent over it she gave a little sigh of pleasure.

"Why, it's a mirror!" she cried; for she could see all her pretty face and fluffy, rainbow-tinted gown reflected in the pool, as natural as life.

Dorothy bent over, too, and began to arrange her hair, blown by the desert wind into straggling tangles. Button-Bright leaned over the edge next, and then began to cry, for the sight of his fox head frightened the poor little fellow.

"I guess I won't look," remarked the shaggy man, sadly, for he didn't like his donkey head, either. While Polly and Dorothy tried to comfort Button-Bright, the shaggy man sat down near the edge of the pool, where his image could not be reflected, and stared at the water thoughtfully. As he did this he noticed a silver plate fastened to a rock just under the surface of the water, and on the silver plate was engraved these words:

THE TRUTH POND

"Ah!" cried the shaggy man, springing to his feet with eager joy; "we've found it at last."

"Found what?" asked Dorothy, running to him.

"The Truth Pond. Now, at last, I may get rid of this frightful head; for we were told, you remember, that only the Truth Pond could restore to me my proper face."

"Me, too!" shouted Button-Bright, trotting up to them.

"Of course," said Dorothy. "It will cure you both of your bad heads, I guess. Isn't it lucky we found it?"

"It is, indeed," replied the shaggy man. "I hated dreadfully to go to Princess Ozma looking like this; and she's to have a birthday celebration, too."

Just then a splash startled them, for Button-Bright, in his anxiety to see the pool that would "cure" him, had stepped too near the edge and tumbled heels over head into the water. Down he went, out of sight entirely, so that only his sailor hat floated on the top of the Truth Pond.

He soon bobbed up, and the shaggy man seized him by his sailor collar and dragged him to the shore, dripping and gasping for breath. They all looked upon the boy wonderingly, for the fox head with its sharp nose and pointed ears was gone, and in its place appeared the chubby round face and blue eyes and pretty curls that had belonged to Button-Bright before King Dox of Foxville transformed him.

"Oh, what a darling!" cried Polly, and would have hugged the little one had he not been so wet.

Their joyful exclamations made the child rub the water out of his eyes and look at his friends questioningly.

"You're all right now, dear," said Dorothy. "Come and look at yourself." She led him to the pool, and although there were still a few ripples

THE SHAGGY MAN'S OWN HEAD RESTORED

on the surface of the water he could see his reflection plainly.

"It's me!" he said, in a pleased yet awed whisper.

" 'Course it is," replied the girl; "and we're all as glad as you are, Button-Bright."

"Well," announced the shaggy man, "it's my turn next." He took off his shaggy coat and laid it on the grass and dived head first into the Truth Pond.

When he came up the donkey head had disappeared, and the shaggy man's own shaggy head was in its place, with the water dripping in little streams from his shaggy whiskers. He scrambled ashore and shook himself to get off some of the wet, and then leaned over the pool to look admiringly at his reflected face.

"I may not be strictly beautiful, even now," he said to his companions, who watched him with smiling faces; "but I'm so much handsomer than any donkey that I feel as proud as I can be."

"You're all right, Shaggy Man," declared Dorothy. "And Button-Bright is all right, too. So let's thank the Truth Pond for being so nice, and start on our journey to the Emerald City."

"I hate to leave it," murmured the shaggy man, with a sigh. "A truth pond wouldn't be a bad thing to carry around with us." But he put on his coat and started with the others in search of some one to direct them on their way.

Tik-Tok and Billina

THEY had not walked far across the flower-strewn meadows when they came upon a fine road leading toward the northwest and winding gracefully among the pretty yellow hills.

"That way," said Dorothy, "must be the direction of the Emerald City. We'd better follow the road until we meet some one or come to a house."

The sun soon dried Button-Bright's sailor suit and the shaggy man's shaggy clothes, and so pleased were they at regaining their own heads that they did not mind at all the brief discomfort of getting wet.

"It's good to be able to whistle again," remarked the shaggy man, "for those donkey lips were so thick I could not whistle a note with them." He warbled a tune as merrily as any bird.

"You'll look more natural at the birthday celebration, too," said Dorothy, happy in seeing her friends so happy.

Polychrome was dancing ahead in her usual sprightly manner, whirling gaily along the smooth, level road, until she passed from sight around the curve of one of the mounds. Suddenly they heard her exclaim "Oh!" and she appeared again, running toward them at full speed.

"What's the matter, Polly?" asked Dorothy, perplexed.

There was no need for the Rainbow's Daughter to answer, for turning the bend in the road there came advancing slowly toward them a funny round man made of burnished copper, gleaming brightly in the sun. Perched on the copper man's shoulder sat a yellow hen, with fluffy feathers and a pearl necklace around her throat.

"Oh, Tik-tok!" cried Dorothy, running forward. When she came to him the copper man lifted the little girl in his copper arms and kissed her cheek with his copper lips.

"Oh, Billina!" cried Dorothy, in a glad voice,

and the yellow hen flew to her arms, to be hugged and petted by turns.

The others were curiously crowding around the group, and the girl said to them:

"It's Tik-tok and Billina; and oh! I'm so glad to see them again."

"Wel-come to Oz," said the copper man, in a monotonous voice.

Dorothy sat right down in the road, the yellow hen in her arms, and began to stroke Billina's back. Said the hen:

"Dorothy, dear, I've some wonderful news to tell you."

"Tell it quick, Billina!" said the girl.

Just then Toto, who had been growling to himself in a cross way, gave a sharp bark and flew at the yellow hen, who ruffled her feathers and let out such an angry screech that Dorothy was startled.

"Stop, Toto! Stop that this minute!" she commanded. "Can't you see that Billina is my friend?" In spite of this warning had she not grabbed Toto quickly by the neck the little dog would have done the yellow hen a mischief, and even now he struggled madly to escape Dorothy's grasp. She slapped his ears once or twice and told him to behave, and the yellow hen flew to Tik-tok's shoulder again, where she was safe.

"What a brute!" croaked Billina, glaring down at the little dog.

"Toto isn't a brute," replied Dorothy; "but at home Uncle Henry has to whip him sometimes for chasing the chickens. Now, look here, Toto," she added, holding up her finger and speaking sternly to him, "you've got to understand that Billina is one of my dearest friends, and mustn't be hurt—now or ever."

Toto wagged his tail as if he understood.

"The miserable thing can't talk," said Billina, with a sneer.

"Yes, he can," replied Dorothy; "he talks with his tail, and I know everything he says. If you could wag your tail, Billina, you wouldn't need words to talk with."

"Nonsense!" said Billina.

"It isn't nonsense at all. Just now Toto says

he's sorry, and that he'll try to love you for my sake. Don't you, Toto?"

"Bow-wow!" said Toto, wagging his tail again.

"But I've such wonderful news for you, Dorothy," cried the yellow hen; "I've——"

"Wait a minute, dear," interrupted the little girl; "I've got to introduce you all, first. That's manners, Billina. This," turning to her traveling companions, "is Mr. Tik-tok, who works by machinery, 'cause his thoughts wind up, and his talk winds up, and his action winds up—like a clock."

"Do they all wind up together?" asked the shaggy man.

"No; each one separate. But he works just lovely, and Tik-tok was a good friend to me once, and saved my life—and Billina's life, too."

"Is he alive?" asked Button-Bright, looking hard at the copper man.

"Oh, no, but his machinery makes him just as good as alive." She turned to the copper man and said politely: "Mr. Tik-tok, these are my new friends: the shaggy man, and Polly the Rainbow's Daughter, and Button-Bright, and Toto. Only Toto isn't a new friend, 'cause he's been to Oz before."

The copper man bowed low, removing his copper hat as he did so.

"I'm ve-ry pleased to meet Dor-o-thy's fr-r-r-r-r——" Here he stopped short.

"Oh, I guess his speech needs winding!" said the little girl, running behind the copper man to get the key off a hook at his back. She wound him up at a place under his right arm and he went on to say:

"Par-don me for run-ning down. I was a-bout to say I am pleased to meet Dor-o-thy's friends, who must be my friends." The words were somewhat jerky, but plain to understand.

"And this is Billina," continued Dorothy, introducing the yellow hen, and they all bowed to her in turn.

"I've such wonderful news," said the hen, turning her head so that one bright eye looked full at Dorothy.

"What is it, dear?" asked the girl.

"I've hatched out ten of the loveliest chicks you ever saw."

"Oh, how nice! And where are they, Billina?"

"I left them at home. But they're beauties, I assure you, and all wonderfully clever. I've named them Dorothy."

"Which one?" asked the girl.

"All of them," replied Billina.

"That's funny. Why did you name them all with the same name?"

"It was so hard to tell them apart," explained the hen. "Now, when I call 'Dorothy,' they all come running to me in a bunch; it's much easier, after all, than having a separate name for each."

"I'm just dying to see 'em, Billina," said Dorothy, eagerly. "But tell me, my friends, how did you happen to be here, in the Country of the Winkies, the first of all to meet us?"

"I'll tell you," answered Tik-tok, in his monotonous voice, all the sounds of his words being on one level—"Prin-cess Oz-ma saw you in her mag-ic pic-ture, and knew you were com-ing here; so she sent Bil-lin-a and me to wel-come you, as she could not come her-self; so that—fiz-i-dig-le cum-so-lut-ing hy-ber-gob-ble in-tu-zib-ick——"

"Good gracious! Whatever's the matter now?"

148

cried Dorothy, as the copper man continued to babble these unmeaning words, which no one could understand at all because they had no sense.

"Don't know," said Button-Bright, who was half scared. Polly whirled away to a distance and turned to look at the copper man in a fright.

"His thoughts have run down, this time," remarked Billina composedly, as she sat on Tik-tok's shoulder and pruned her sleek feathers. "When he can't think he can't talk properly, any more than you can. You'll have to wind up his thoughts, Dorothy, or else I'll have to finish his story myself."

Dorothy ran around and got the key again and wound up Tik-tok under his left arm, after which he could speak plainly again.

"Par-don me," he said, "but when my thoughts run down my speech has no mean-ing, for words are formed on-ly by thought. I was a-bout to say that Oz-ma sent us to wel-come you and in-vite you to come straight to the Em-er-ald Ci-ty. She was too bus-y to come her-self, for she is pre-par-ing for her birth-day cel-e-bra-tion, which is to be a grand af-fair."

"I've heard of it," said Dorothy, "and I'm glad we've come in time to attend. Is it far from here to the Emerald City?"

"Not ve-ry far," answered Tik-tok, "and we have plen-ty of time. To-night we will stop at the pal-ace of the Tin Wood-man, and to-mor-row night we will ar-rive at the Em-er-ald Ci-ty."

"Goody!" cried Dorothy. "I'd like to see dear Nick Chopper again. How's his heart?"

"It's fine," said Billina; "the Tin Woodman says it gets softer and kindlier every day. He's waiting at his castle to welcome you, Dorothy; but he couldn't come with us because he's get-ting polished as bright as possible for Ozma's party."

"Well, then," said Dorothy, "let's start on, and we can talk more as we go."

They proceeded on their journey in a friendly group, for Polychrome had discovered that the copper man was harmless and was no longer afraid of him. Button-Bright was also reassured, and took quite a fancy to Tik-tok. He wanted the clockwork man to open himself, so that he might see the wheels go round; but that was a thing Tik-tok could not do. Button-Bright then wanted to wind up the copper man, and Dorothy promised he should do so as soon as any part of the machinery ran down. This pleased Button-Bright, who held fast to one of Tik-tok's copper hands as he trudged along the road, while Doro-thy walked on the other side of her old friend and Billina perched by turns upon his shoulder or his copper hat. Polly once more joyously danced ahead and Toto ran after her, barking with glee. The shaggy man was left to walk behind; but he didn't seem to mind that a bit, and whistled merrily or looked curiously upon the pretty scenes they passed.

At last they came to a hilltop from which the tin castle of Nick Chopper could plainly be seen, its towers glistening magnificently under the rays of the declining sun.

"How pretty!" exclaimed Dorothy. "I've never seen the Emp'ror's new house before."

"He built it because the old castle was damp, and likely to rust his tin body," said Billina. "All those towers and steeples and domes and gables took a lot of tin, as you can see."

"Is it a toy?" asked Button-Bright, softly.

"No, dear," answered Dorothy; "it's better than that. It's the fairy dwelling of a fairy prince."

The Emperor's Tin Castle

THE grounds around Nick Chopper's new house were laid out in pretty flower-beds, with fountains of crystal water and statues of tin representing the Emperor's personal friends. Dorothy was astonished and delighted to find a tin statue of herself standing on a tin pedestal at a bend in the avenue leading up to the entrance. It was life-size and showed her in her sunbonnet with her basket on her arm, just as she had first appeared in the Land of Oz.

"Oh, Toto—you're there too!" she exclaimed; and sure enough there was the tin figure of Toto lying at the tin Dorothy's feet.

Also Dorothy saw figures of the Scarecrow, and the Wizard, and Ozma, and of many others, including Tik-tok. They reached the grand tin

entrance to the tin castle, and the Tin Woodman himself came running out of the door to embrace little Dorothy and give her a glad welcome. He welcomed her friends as well, and the Rainbow's Daughter he declared to be the loveliest vision his tin eyes had ever beheld. He patted Button-Bright's curly head tenderly, for he was fond of children, and turned to the shaggy man and shook both his hands at the same time.

Nick Chopper, the Emperor of the Winkies, who was also known throughout the Land of Oz as the Tin Woodman, was certainly a remarkable person. He was neatly made, all of tin, nicely soldered at the joints, and his various limbs were cleverly hinged to his body so that he could use them nearly as well as if they had been common flesh. Once, he told the shaggy man, he had been made all of flesh and bones, as other people are, and then he chopped wood in the forests to earn his living. But the axe slipped so often and cut off parts of him—which he had replaced with tin—that finally there was no flesh left, nothing but tin; so he became a real tin woodman. The wonderful Wizard of Oz had given him an excellent heart to replace his old one, and he didn't at all mind being tin. Every one loved him, he loved every one; and he was therefore as happy as the day was long.

The Emperor was proud of his new tin castle, and showed his visitors through all the rooms. Every bit of the furniture was made of brightly polished tin—the tables, chairs, beds, and all—even the floors and walls were of tin.

"I suppose," said he, "that there are no cleverer tinsmiths in all the world than the Winkies. It would be hard to match this castle in Kansas; wouldn't it, little Dorothy?"

"Very hard," replied the child, gravely.

"It must have cost a lot of money," remarked the shaggy man.

"Money! Money in Oz!" cried the Tin Woodman. "What a queer idea! Did you suppose we are so vulgar as to use money here?"

"Why not?" asked the shaggy man.

"If we used money to buy things with, instead

of love and kindness and the desire to please one another, then we should be no better than the rest of the world," declared the Tin Woodman. "Fortunately money is not known in the Land of Oz at all. We have no rich, and no poor; for what one wishes the others all try to give him, in order to make him happy, and no one in all Oz cares to have more than he can use."

"Good!" cried the shaggy man, greatly pleased to hear this. "I also despise money—a man in Butterfield owes me fifteen cents, and I will not take it from him. The Land of Oz is surely the most favored land in all the world, and its people the happiest. I should like to live here always."

The Tin Woodman listened with respectful attention. Already he loved the shaggy man, although he did not yet know of the Love Magnet. So he said:

"If you can prove to the Princess Ozma that you are honest and true and worthy of our friendship, you may indeed live here all your days, and be as happy as we are."

"I'll try to prove that," said the shaggy man, earnestly.

"And now," continued the Emperor, "you must all go to your rooms and prepare for dinner, which will presently be served in the grand tin dining-hall. I am sorry, Shaggy Man, that I can not offer you a change of clothing; but I dress only in tin, myself, and I suppose that would not suit you."

"I care little about dress," said the shaggy man, indifferently.

"So I should imagine," replied the Emperor, with true politeness.

They were shown to their rooms and permitted to make such toilets as they could, and soon they assembled again in the grand tin dining-hall, even Toto being present. For the Emperor was fond of Dorothy's little dog, and the girl explained to her friends that in Oz all animals were treated with as much consideration as the people—"if they behave themselves," she added.

Toto behaved himself, and sat in a tin high-chair beside Dorothy and ate his dinner from a tin platter.

Indeed, they all ate from tin dishes, but these were of pretty shapes and brightly polished; Dorothy thought they were just as good as silver.

Button-Bright looked curiously at the man who had "no appetite inside him," for the Tin Woodman, although he had prepared so fine a feast for his guests, ate not a mouthful himself, sitting patiently in his place to see that all built so they could eat were well and plentifully served.

What pleased Button-Bright most about the

POLYCHROME DANCED GRACEFULLY
TO THE MUSIC

dinner was the tin orchestra that played sweet music while the company ate. The players were not tin, being just ordinary Winkies; but the instruments they played upon were all tin—tin trumpets, tin fiddles, tin drums and cymbals and flutes and horns and all. They played so nicely the "Shining Emperor Waltz," composed expressly in honor of the Tin Woodman by Mr. H. M. Woggle-Bug, T. E., that Polly could not resist dancing to it. After she had tasted a few dewdrops, freshly gathered for her, she danced gracefully to the music while the others finished their repast; and when she whirled until her fleecy draperies of rainbow hues enveloped her like a cloud, the Tin Woodman was so delighted that he clapped his tin hands until the noise of them drowned the sound of the cymbals.

Altogether it was a merry meal, although Polychrome ate little and the host nothing at all.

"I'm sorry the Rainbow's Daughter missed her mist-cakes," said the Tin Woodman to Dorothy; "but by a mistake Miss Polly's mist-cakes were mislaid and not missed until now. I'll try to have some for her breakfast."

They spent the evening telling stories, and the next morning left the splendid tin castle and set out upon the road to the Emerald City. The Tin Woodman went with them, of course, having by this time been so brightly polished that

he sparkled like silver. His axe, which he always
carried with him, had a steel blade that was tin
plated and a handle covered with tin plate beautifully engraved and set with diamonds.

The Winkies assembled before the castle gates
and cheered their Emperor as he marched away,
and it was easy to see that they all loved him
dearly.

Visiting the Pumpkin-Field

DOROTHY let Button-Bright wind up the clock-work in the copper man this morning—his thinking machine first, then his speech, and finally his action; so he would doubtless run perfectly until they had reached the Emerald City. The copper man and the tin man were good friends, and not so much alike as you might think. For one was alive and the other moved by means of machinery; one was tall and angular and the other short and round. You could love the Tin Woodman because he had a fine nature, kindly and simple; but the machine man you could only admire without loving, since to love such a thing as he was as impossible as to love a sewing-machine or an automobile. Yet Tik-tok was popular with the people of Oz because he was so trustworthy, reliable and true; he was sure to do exactly what he was wound up to do, at all times and in all circumstances. Perhaps it is better to be a machine that does its duty than a flesh-and-blood person who will not, for a dead truth is better than a live falsehood.

About noon the travelers reached a large field of pumpkins—a vegetable quite appropriate to the yellow country of the Winkies—and some of the pumpkins which grew there were of remarkable size. Just before they entered upon this field they saw three little mounds that looked like graves, with a pretty headstone to each one of them.

"What is this?" asked Dorothy, in wonder.

"It's Jack Pumpkinhead's private graveyard," replied the Tin Woodman.

"But I thought nobody ever died in Oz," she said.

"Nor do they; although if one is bad, he may be condemned and killed by the good citizens," he answered.

Dorothy ran over to the little graves and read the words engraved upon the tombstones. The first one said:

> **Here Lies the Mortal Part of**
> **JACK PUMPKINHEAD**
> **Which Spoiled April 9th.**

She then went to the next stone, which read:

> **Here Lies the Mortal Part of**
> **JACK PUMPKINHEAD**
> **Which Spoiled October 2nd.**

On the third stone were carved these words:

> **Here Lies the Mortal Part of**
> **JACK PUMPKINHEAD**
> **Which Spoiled January 24th.**

"Poor Jack!" sighed Dorothy. "I'm sorry he had to die in three parts, for I hoped to see him again."

"So you shall," declared the Tin Woodman, "since he is still alive. Come with me to his house, for Jack is now a farmer and lives in this very pumpkin field."

They walked over to a monstrous big, hollow pumpkin which had a door and windows cut through the rind. There was a stovepipe running through the stem, and six steps had been built leading up to the front door.

They walked up to this door and looked in. Seated on a bench was a man clothed in a spotted shirt, a red vest, and faded blue trousers, whose body was merely sticks of wood, jointed clumsily together. On his neck was set a round, yellow pumpkin, with a face carved on it such as a boy often carves on a jack-lantern.

This queer man was engaged in snapping slippery pumpkin-seeds with his wooden fingers, trying to hit a target on the other side of the room with them. He did not know he had visitors until Dorothy exclaimed:

"Why, it's Jack Pumpkinhead himself!"

He turned and saw them, and at once came forward to greet the little Kansas girl and Nick Chopper, and to be introduced to their new friends.

CALLING ON JACK PUMPKINHEAD

Button-Bright was at first rather shy with the quaint Pumpkinhead, but Jack's face was so jolly and smiling—being carved that way—that the boy soon grew to like him.

"I thought, a while ago, that you were buried in three parts," said Dorothy; "but now I see you're just the same as ever."

"Not quite the same, my dear, for my mouth is a little more one-sided than it used to be; but pretty nearly the same. I've a new head, and this is the fourth one I've owned since Ozma first made me and brought me to life by sprinkling me with the Magic Powder."

"What became of the other heads, Jack?"

"They spoiled and I buried them, for they were not even fit for pies. Each time Ozma has carved me a new head just like the old one, and as my body is by far the largest part of me I am still Jack Pumpkinhead, no matter how often I change my upper end. Once we had a dreadful time to find another pumpkin, as they were out of season, and so I was obliged to wear my old head a little longer than was strictly healthy. But after this sad experience I resolved to raise pumpkins myself, so as never to be caught again without one handy; and now I have this fine field that you see before you. Some grow pretty big—too big to be used for heads—so I dug out this one and use it for a house."

"Isn't it damp?" asked Dorothy.

"Not very. There isn't much left but the shell, you see, and it will last a long time yet."

"I think you are brighter than you used to be, Jack," said the Tin Woodman. "Your last head was a stupid one."

"The seeds in this one are better," was the reply.

"Are you going to Ozma's party?" asked Dorothy.

"Yes," said he; "I wouldn't miss it for anything. Ozma's my parent, you know, because she built my body and carved my pumpkin head. I'll follow you to the Emerald City to-morrow, where we shall meet again. I can't go to-day, because I have to plant fresh pumpkin-seeds and water the young vines. But give my love to

Ozma, and tell her I'll be there in time for the jubilation."

"We will," she promised; and then they all left him and resumed their journey.

THE neat yellow houses of the Winkies were now to be seen standing here and there along the roadway, giving the country a more cheerful and civilized look. They were farm-houses, though, and set far apart; for in the Land of Oz there were no towns or villages except the magnificent Emerald City in its center.

Hedges of evergreen or of yellow roses bordered the broad highway and the farms showed the care of their industrious inhabitants. The nearer the travelers came to the great city the more prosperous the country became, and they crossed many bridges over the sparkling streams and rivulets that watered the lands.

As they walked leisurely along the shaggy man said to the Tin Woodman:

"What sort of a Magic Powder was it, that made your friend the Pumpkinhead live?"

"It was called the Powder of Life," was the answer; "and it was invented by a crooked Sorcerer who lived in the mountains of the North Country. A Witch named Mombi got some of this powder from the crooked Sorcerer and took it home with her. Ozma lived with the Witch then, for it was before she became our Princess, while Mombi had transformed her into the shape of a boy. Well, while Mombi was gone to the crooked Sorcerer's, the boy made this pumpkin-headed man to amuse himself, and also with the hope of frightening the Witch with it when she returned. But Mombi was not scared, and she sprinkled the Pumpkinhead with her Magic Powder of Life, to see if the Powder would work. Ozma was watching, and saw the Pumpkinhead come to life; so that night she took the pepper-box containing the Powder and ran away with it and with Jack, in search of adventures.

"Next day they found a wooden Saw-Horse standing by the roadside, and sprinkled it with the Powder. It came to life at once, and Jack Pumpkinhead rode the Saw-Horse to the Emerald City."

"What became of the Saw-Horse, afterward?"

asked the shaggy man, much interested in this story.

"Oh, it's alive yet, and you will probably meet it presently in the Emerald City. Afterward Ozma used the last of the Powder to bring the Flying Gump to life; but as soon as it had carried her away from her enemies the Gump was taken apart, so it doesn't exist any more."

"It's too bad the Powder of Life was all used up," remarked the shaggy man; "it would be a handy thing to have around."

"I am not so sure of that, sir," answered the Tin Woodman. "A while ago the crooked Sorcerer who invented the Magic Powder fell down a precipice and was killed. All his possessions went to a relative—an old woman named Dyna, who lives in the Emerald City. She went to the mountains where the Sorcerer had lived and brought away everything she thought of value. Among them was a small bottle of the Powder of Life; but of course Dyna didn't know it was a Magic Powder, at all. It happened she had once had a big blue bear for a pet; but the bear choked to death on a fishbone one day, and she loved it so dearly that Dyna made a rug of its skin, leaving the head and four paws on the hide. She kept the rug on the floor of her front parlor."

"I've seen rugs like that," said the shaggy man, nodding, "but never one made from a blue bear."

"Well," continued the Tin Woodman, "the old woman had an idea that the Powder in the bottle must be moth-powder, because it smelled something like moth-powder; so one day she sprinkled it on her bear rug to keep the moths out of it. She said, looking lovingly at the skin: 'I wish my dear bear were alive again!' To her horror the bear rug at once came to life, having been sprinkled with the Magic Powder; and now this live bear rug is a great trial to her, and makes her a lot of trouble."

"Why?" asked the shaggy man.

"Well, it stands up on its four feet and walks all around, and gets in the way; and that spoils it for a rug. It can't speak, although it is alive;

for, while its head might say words, it has no breath in a solid body to push the words out of its mouth. It's a very slimpsy affair altogether, that bear rug, and the old woman is sorry it came to life. Every day she has to scold it, and make it lie down flat on the parlor floor to be walked upon; but sometimes when she goes to market the rug will hump up its back skin, and stand on its four feet, and trot along after her."

"I should think Dyna would like that," said Dorothy.

"Well, she doesn't; because every one knows it isn't a real bear, but just a hollow skin, and so of no actual use in the world except for a rug," answered the Tin Woodman. "Therefore I believe it is a good thing that all the Magic

Powder of Life is now used up, as it can not cause any more trouble."

"Perhaps you're right," said the shaggy man, thoughtfully.

At noon they stopped at a farm-house, where it delighted the farmer and his wife to be able to give them a good luncheon. The farm people knew Dorothy, having seen her when she was in the country before, and they treated the little girl with as much respect as they did the Emperor, because she was a friend of the powerful Princess Ozma.

They had not proceeded far after leaving this farm-house before coming to a high bridge over a broad river. This river, the Tin Woodman informed them, was the boundary between the Country of the Winkies and the territory of the Emerald City. The city itself was still a long way off, but all around it was a green meadow, as pretty as a well-kept lawn, and in this were neither houses nor farms to spoil the beauty of the scene.

From the top of the high bridge they could see far away the magnificent spires and splendid domes of the superb city, sparkling like brilliant jewels as they towered above the emerald walls. The shaggy man drew a deep breath of awe and amazement, for never had he dreamed that such a grand and beautiful place could exist—even in the fairyland of Oz.

Polly was so pleased that her violet eyes sparkled like amethysts, and she danced away from her companions across the bridge and into a group of feathery trees lining both the roadsides. These trees she stopped to look at with pleasure and surprise, for their leaves were shaped like ostrich plumes, their feather edges beautifully curled; and all the plumes were tinted in the same dainty rainbow hues that appeared in Polychrome's own pretty gauze gown.

"Father ought to see these trees," she murmured; "they are almost as lovely as his own rainbows."

Then she gave a start of terror, for beneath the trees came stalking two great beasts, either one big enough to crush the little Daughter of the Rainbow with one blow of his paws, or to eat her up with one snap of his enormous jaws. One was a tawny lion, as tall as a horse, nearly; the other a striped tiger almost the same size.

Polly was too frightened to scream or to stir; she stood still with a wildly beating heart until Dorothy rushed past her and with a glad cry threw her arms around the huge lion's neck, hugging and kissing the beast with evident joy.

"Oh, I'm *so* glad to see you again!" cried the

DOROTHY THREW HER ARMS AROUND
THE LION'S NECK

little Kansas girl. "And the Hungry Tiger, too! How fine you're both looking. Are you well and happy?"

"We certainly are, Dorothy," answered the Lion, in a deep voice that sounded pleasant and kind; "and we are greatly pleased that you have come to Ozma's party. It's going to be a grand affair, I promise you."

"There will be lots of fat babies at the celebration, I hear," remarked the Hungry Tiger, yawning so that his mouth opened dreadfully wide and showed all his big, sharp teeth; "but of course I can't eat any of 'em."

"Is your Conscience still in good order?" asked Dorothy, anxiously.

"Yes; it rules me like a tyrant," answered the Tiger, sorrowfully. "I can imagine nothing more unpleasant than to own a Conscience," and he winked slyly at his friend the Lion.

"You're fooling me!" said Dorothy, with a laugh. "I don't b'lieve you'd eat a baby if you lost your Conscience. Come here, Polly," she called, "and be introduced to my friends."

Polly advanced rather shyly.

"You have some queer friends, Dorothy," she said.

"The queerness doesn't matter, so long as they're friends," was the answer. "This is the Cowardly Lion, who isn't a coward at all, but just thinks he is. The Wizard gave him some courage once, and he has part of it left."

The Lion bowed with great dignity to Polly.

"You are very lovely, my dear," said he. "I hope we shall be friends when we are better acquainted."

"And this is the Hungry Tiger," continued Dorothy. "He says he longs to eat fat babies; but the truth is he is never hungry at all, 'cause he gets plenty to eat; and I don't s'pose he'd hurt anybody even if he *was* hungry."

"Hush, Dorothy," whispered the Tiger; "you'll ruin my reputation if you are not more discreet. It isn't what we are, but what folks think we are, that counts in this world. And come to think of it Miss Polly would make a fine variegated breakfast, I'm sure."

The Emerald City

THE others now came up, and the Tin Woodman greeted the Lion and the Tiger cordially. Button-Bright yelled with fear when Dorothy first took his hand and led him toward the great beasts; but the girl insisted they were kind and good, and so the boy mustered up courage enough to pat their heads; after they had spoken to him gently and he had looked into their intelligent eyes his fear vanished entirely and he was so delighted with the animals that he wanted to keep close to them and stroke their soft fur every minute.

As for the shaggy man, he might have been afraid if he had met the beasts alone, or in any other country; but so many were the marvels in the Land of Oz that he was no longer easily surprised, and Dorothy's friendship for the Lion and Tiger was enough to assure him they were safe companions. Toto barked at the Cowardly Lion in joyous greeting, for he knew the beast of old and loved him, and it was funny to see how gently the Lion raised his huge paw to pat Toto's head. The little dog smelled of the Tiger's nose and the Tiger politely shook paws with him; so they were quite likely to become firm friends.

Tik-tok and Billina knew the beasts well, so merely bade them good day and asked after their healths and inquired about the Princess Ozma.

Now it was seen that the Cowardly Lion and the Hungry Tiger were drawing behind them a splendid golden chariot, to which they were harnessed by golden cords. The body of the chariot was decorated on the outside with designs in clusters of sparkling emeralds, while inside it was lined with a green and gold satin, and the cushions of the seats were of green plush embroidered in gold with a crown, underneath which was a monogram.

"Why, it's Ozma's own royal chariot!" exclaimed Dorothy.

"Yes," said the Cowardly Lion; "Ozma sent us to meet you here, for she feared you would be weary with your long walk and she wished

you to enter the City in a style becoming your exalted rank."

"What!" cried Polly, looking at Dorothy curiously. "Do you belong to the nobility?"

"Just in Oz I do," said the child, " 'cause Ozma made me a Princess, you know. But when I'm home in Kansas I'm only a country girl, and have to help with the churning and wipe the dishes while Aunt Em washes 'em. Do you have to help wash dishes on the rainbow, Polly?"

"No, dear," answered Polychrome, smiling.

"Well, I don't have to work any in Oz, either," said Dorothy. "It's kind of fun to be a Princess once in a while; don't you think so?"

"Dorothy and Polychrome and Button-Bright

are all to ride in the chariot," said the Lion. "So get in, my dears, and be careful not to mar the gold or put your dusty feet on the embroidery."

Button-Bright was delighted to ride behind such a superb team, and he told Dorothy it made him feel like an actor in a circus. As the strides of the animals brought them nearer to the Emerald City every one bowed respectfully to the children, as well as to the Tin Woodman, Tiktok, and the shaggy man, who were following behind.

The Yellow Hen had perched upon the back of the chariot, where she could tell Dorothy more about her wonderful chickens as they rode. And so the grand chariot came finally to the high wall surrounding the City, and paused before the magnificent jewel-studded gates.

These were opened by a cheerful-looking little man who wore green spectacles over his eyes. Dorothy introduced him to her friends as the Guardian of the Gates, and they noticed a big bunch of keys suspended on the golden chain that hung around his neck. The chariot passed through the outer gates into a fine arched chamber built in the thick wall, and through the inner gates into the streets of the Emerald City.

Polychrome exclaimed in rapture at the wondrous beauty that met her eyes on every side as they rode through this stately and imposing

City, the equal of which has never been discovered, even in Fairyland. Button-Bright could only say "My!" so amazing was the sight; but his eyes were wide open and he tried to look in every direction at the same time, so as not to miss anything.

The shaggy man was fairly astounded at what he saw, for the graceful and handsome buildings were covered with plates of gold and set with emeralds so splendid and valuable that in any other part of the world any one of them would have been worth a fortune to its owner. The sidewalks were superb marble slabs polished as smooth as glass, and the curbs that separated the walks from the broad street were also set thick with clustered emeralds. There were many people on these walks—men, women, and children—all dressed in handsome garments of silk or satin or velvet, with beautiful jewels. Better even than this: all seemed happy and contented, for their faces were smiling and free from care, and music and laughter might be heard on every side.

"Don't they work, at all?" asked the shaggy man.

"To be sure they work," replied the Tin Woodman; "this fair city could not be built or cared for without labor, nor could the fruit and vegetables and other food be provided for the inhabitants to eat. But no one works more than half his time, and the people of Oz enjoy their labors as much as they do their play."

"It's wonderful!" declared the shaggy man. "I do hope Ozma will let me live here."

The chariot, winding through many charming streets, paused before a building so vast and noble and elegant that even Button-Bright guessed at once that it was the Royal Palace. Its gardens and ample grounds were surrounded by a separate wall, not so high or thick as the wall around the City, but more daintily designed and built all of green marble. The gates flew open as the chariot appeared before them, and the Cowardly Lion and Hungry Tiger trotted up a jeweled driveway to the front door of the palace and stopped short.

"Here we are!" said Dorothy, gaily, and helped Button-Bright from the chariot. Polychrome leaped out lightly after them, and they were greeted by a crowd of gorgeously dressed servants who bowed low as the visitors mounted the marble steps. At their head was a pretty little maid with dark hair and eyes, dressed all in green embroidered with silver. Dorothy ran up to her with evident pleasure, and exclaimed:

"O Jellia Jamb! I'm so glad to see you again. Where's Ozma?"

"In her room, your Highness," replied the little maid demurely, for this was Ozma's favorite attendant. "She wishes you to come to her as soon as you have rested and changed your dress, Princess Dorothy. And you and your friends are to dine with her this evening."

"When is her birthday, Jellia?" asked the girl.

"Day after to-morrow, your Highness."

"And where's the Scarecrow?"

"He's gone into the Munchkin country to get some fresh straw to stuff himself with, in honor of Ozma's celebration," replied the maid. "He returns to the Emerald City to-morrow, he said."

By this time Tik-tok, the Tin Woodman, and the shaggy man had arrived and the chariot had gone around to the back of the palace, Billina going with the Lion and Tiger to see her chick-

"O, JELLIA JAMB! I'M SO GLAD TO SEE YOU"

ens after her absence from them. But Toto stayed close beside Dorothy.

"Come in, please," said Jellia Jamb; "it shall be our pleasant duty to escort all of you to the rooms prepared for your use."

The shaggy man hesitated. Dorothy had never known him to be ashamed of his shaggy looks before, but now that he was surrounded by so much magnificence and splendor the shaggy man felt sadly out of place.

Dorothy assured him that all her friends were welcome at Ozma's palace, so he carefully dusted his shaggy shoes with his shaggy handkerchief and entered the grand hall after the others.

Tik-tok lived at the Royal Palace and the Tin Woodman always had the same room whenever he visited Ozma, so these two went at once to

remove the dust of the journey from their shining bodies. Dorothy also had a pretty suite of rooms which she always occupied when in the Emerald City; but several servants walked ahead politely to show the way, although she was quite sure she could find the rooms herself. She took Button-Bright with her, because he seemed too small to be left alone in such a big palace; but Jellia Jamb herself ushered the beautiful Daughter of the Rainbow to her apartments, because it was easy to see that Polychrome was used to splendid palaces and was therefore entitled to especial attention.

The Shaggy Man's Welcome

THE shaggy man stood in the great hall, his shaggy hat in his hands, wondering what would become of him. He had never been a guest in a fine palace before; perhaps he had never been a guest anywhere. In the big, cold, outside world people did not invite shaggy men to their homes, and this shaggy man of ours had slept more in hay-lofts and stables than in comfortable rooms. When the others left the great hall he eyed the splendidly dressed servants of the Princess Ozma as if he expected to be ordered out; but one of them bowed before him as respectfully as if he had been a prince, and said:

"Permit me, sir, to conduct you to your apartments."

The shaggy man drew a long breath and took courage.

"Very well," he answered; "I'm ready."

Through the big hall they went, up the grand staircase carpeted thick with velvet, and so along a wide corridor to a carved doorway. Here the servant paused, and opening the door said with polite deference:

"Be good enough to enter, sir, and make yourself at home in the rooms our Royal Ozma has ordered prepared for you. Whatever you see is for you to use and enjoy, as if your own. The Princess dines at seven, and I shall be here in time to lead you to the drawing-room, where you will be privileged to meet the lovely Ruler of Oz. Is there any command, in the meantime, with which you desire to honor me?"

"No," said the shaggy man; "but I'm much obliged."

He entered the room and shut the door, and for a time stood in bewilderment, admiring the grandeur before him.

He had been given one of the handsomest apartments in the most magnificent palace in the world, and you can not wonder that his good fortune astonished and awed him until he grew used to his surroundings.

The furniture was upholstered in cloth of gold, with the royal crown embroidered upon it in scarlet. The rug upon the marble floor was so thick and soft that he could not hear the sound of his own footsteps, and upon the walls were splendid tapestries woven with scenes from the Land of Oz. Books and ornaments were scattered about in profusion, and the shaggy man thought he had never seen so many pretty things in one place before. In one corner played a tinkling fountain of perfumed water, and in another was a table bearing a golden tray loaded with freshly gathered fruit, including several of the red-cheeked apples that the shaggy man loved.

At the farther end of this charming room was an open doorway, and he crossed over to find himself in a bedroom containing more comforts than the shaggy man had ever before imagined.

The bedstead was of gold and set with many brilliant diamonds, and the coverlet had designs of pearls and rubies sewed upon it. At one side of the bedroom was a dainty dressing-room, with closets containing a large assortment of fresh clothing; and beyond this was the bath—a large room having a marble pool big enough to swim in, with white marble steps leading down to the water. Around the edge of the pool were set rows of fine emeralds as large as door-knobs, while the water of the bath was clear as crystal.

For a time the shaggy man gazed upon all this luxury with silent amazement. Then he decided, being wise in his way, to take advantage of his good fortune. He removed his shaggy boots and his shaggy clothing, and bathed in the pool with rare enjoyment. After he had dried himself with the soft towels he went into the dressing-room and took fresh linen from the drawers and put it on, finding that everything fitted him exactly. He examined the contents of the closets and selected an elegant suit of clothing. Strangely enough, everything about it was shaggy, although so new and beautiful, and he sighed with contentment to realize that he could now be finely dressed and still be the shaggy man. His coat was of rose-colored velvet, trimmed with shags and bobtails, with buttons of blood-red rubies and golden shags around the

THE SHAGGY MAN ADMIRES HIS NEW CLOTHES

edges. His vest was a shaggy satin of a delicate cream color, and his knee-breeches of rose velvet trimmed like the coat. Shaggy creamy stockings of silk, and shaggy slippers of rose leather with ruby buckles, completed his costume, and when he was thus attired the shaggy man looked at himself in a long mirror with great admiration. On a table he found a mother-of-pearl chest decorated with delicate silver vines and flowers of clustered rubies, and on the cover was a silver plate engraved with these words:

THE SHAGGY MAN:

HIS BOX OF ORNAMENTS

The chest was not locked, so he opened it and was almost dazzled by the brilliance of the rich jewels it contained. After admiring the pretty things, he took out a fine golden watch with a big chain, several handsome finger-rings, and an ornament of rubies to pin upon the breast of his shaggy shirt-bosom. Having carefully brushed his hair and whiskers all the wrong way to make them look as shaggy as possible, the shaggy man breathed a deep sigh of joy and decided he was ready to meet the Royal Princess as soon as she sent for him. While he waited he returned to the beautiful sitting room and ate several of the red-cheeked apples to pass away the time.

Meanwhile Dorothy had dressed herself in a pretty gown of soft grey embroidered with silver, and put a blue-and-gold suit of satin upon little Button-Bright, who looked as sweet as a cherub in it. Followed by the boy and Toto—the dog with a new green ribbon around his neck—she hastened down to the splendid drawing-room of the palace, where, seated upon an exquisite throne of carved malachite and nestled amongst its green satin cushions was the lovely Princess Ozma, waiting eagerly to welcome her friend.

Princess Ozma of Oz

THE royal historians of Oz, who are fine writers and know any number of big words, have often tried to describe the rare beauty of Ozma and failed because the words were not good enough. So of course I can not hope to tell you how great was the charm of this little Princess, or how her loveliness put to shame all the sparkling jewels and magnificent luxury that surrounded her in this her royal palace. Whatever else was beautiful or dainty or delightful of itself faded to dullness when contrasted with Ozma's bewitching face, and it has often been said by those who know that no other ruler in all the world can ever hope to equal the gracious charm of her manner.

Everything about Ozma attracted one, and she

inspired love and the sweetest affection rather than awe or ordinary admiration. Dorothy threw her arms around her little friend and hugged and kissed her rapturously, and Toto barked joyfully and Button-Bright smiled a happy smile and consented to sit on the soft cushions close beside the Princess.

"Why didn't you send me word you were going to have a birthday party?" asked the little Kansas girl, when the first greetings were over.

"Didn't I?" asked Ozma, her pretty eyes dancing with merriment.

"Did you?" replied Dorothy, trying to think.

"Who do you imagine, dear, mixed up those roads, so as to start you wandering in the direction of Oz?" inquired the Princess.

"Oh! I never 'spected *you* of that," cried Dorothy.

"I've watched you in my Magic Picture all the way here," declared Ozma, "and twice I thought I should have to use the Magic Belt to save you and transport you to the Emerald City. Once was when the Scoodlers caught you, and again when you reached the Deadly Desert. But the shaggy man was able to help you out both times, so I did not interfere."

"Do you know who Button-Bright is?" asked Dorothy.

"No; I never saw him until you found him

in the road, and then only in my Magic Picture."

"And did you send Polly to us?"

"No, dear; the Rainbow's Daughter slid from her father's pretty arch just in time to meet you."

"Well," said Dorothy, "I've promised King Dox of Foxville and King Kik-a-bray of Dunkiton that I'd ask you to invite them to your party."

"I have already done that," returned Ozma, "because I thought it would please you to favor them."

"Did you 'vite the Musicker?" asked Button-Bright.

"No; because he would be too noisy, and might interfere with the comfort of others. When music is not very good, and is indulged in all the time, it is better that the performer should be alone," said the Princess.

"I like the Musicker's music," declared the boy, gravely.

"But I don't," said Dorothy.

"Well, there will be plenty of music at my celebration," promised Ozma; "so I've an idea Button-Bright won't miss the Musicker at all."

Just then Polychrome danced in, and Ozma rose to greet the Rainbow's Daughter in her sweetest and most cordial manner.

Dorothy thought she had never seen two prettier creatures together than these lovely maidens; but Polly knew at once her own dainty beauty could not match that of Ozma, yet was not a bit jealous because this was so.

The Wizard of Oz was announced, and a dried-up, little, old man, clothed all in black, entered the drawing-room. His face was cheery and his eyes twinkling with humor, so Polly and Button-Bright were not at all afraid of the wonderful personage whose fame as a humbug magician had spread throughout the world. After greeting Dorothy with much affection, he stood modestly behind Ozma's throne and listened to the lively prattle of the young people.

Now the shaggy man appeared, and so startling was his appearance, all clad in shaggy new raiment, that Dorothy cried "Oh!" and clasped her hands impulsively as she examined her friend with pleased eyes.

"He's still shaggy, all right," remarked Button-Bright; and Ozma nodded brightly because she had meant the shaggy man to remain shaggy when she provided his new clothes for him.

Dorothy led him toward the throne, as he was shy in such fine company, and presented him gracefully to the Princess, saying:

"This, your Highness, is my friend, the shaggy man, who owns the Love Magnet."

"You are welcome to Oz," said the girl Ruler, in gracious accents. "But tell me, sir, where did you get the Love Magnet which you say you own?"

The shaggy man grew red and looked downcast, as he answered in a low voice:

"I stole it, your Majesty."

"Oh, Shaggy Man!" cried Dorothy. "How dreadful! And you told me the Eskimo gave you the Love Magnet."

He shuffled first on one foot and then on the other, much embarrassed.

"I told you a falsehood, Dorothy," he said; "but now, having bathed in the Truth Pond, I must tell nothing but the truth."

"Why did you steal it?" asked Ozma, gently.

"Because no one loved me, or cared for me," said the shaggy man, "and I wanted to be loved a great deal. It was owned by a girl in Butterfield who was loved too much, so that the young men quarreled over her, which made her unhappy. After I had stolen the Magnet from her, only one young man continued to love the girl, and she married him and regained her happiness."

"Are you sorry you stole it?" asked the Princess.

"No, your Highness; I'm glad," he answered; "for it has pleased me to be loved, and if Dorothy had not cared for me I could not have accompanied her to this beautiful Land of Oz, or met its kind-hearted Ruler. Now that I'm here, I hope to remain, and to become one of your Majesty's most faithful subjects."

"But in Oz we are loved for ourselves alone,

IN THE ROYAL PALACE OF OZ

and for our kindness to one another, and for our good deeds," she said.

"I'll give up the Love Magnet," said the shaggy man, eagerly; "Dorothy shall have it."

"But every one loves Dorothy already," declared the Wizard.

"Then Button-Bright shall have it."

"Don't want it," said the boy, promptly.

"Then I'll give it to the Wizard, for I'm sure the lovely Princess Ozma does not need it."

"All my people love the Wizard, too," announced the Princess, laughing; "so we will hang the Love Magnet over the gates of the Emerald City, that whoever shall enter or leave the gates may be loved and loving."

"That is a good idea," said the shaggy man; "I agree to it most willingly."

Those assembled now went in to dinner, which you may imagine was a grand affair; and afterward Ozma asked the Wizard to give them an exhibition of his magic.

The Wizard took eight tiny white piglets from an inside pocket and set them on the table. One was dressed like a clown, and performed funny antics, and the others leaped over the spoons and dishes and ran around the table like race-horses, and turned hand-springs and were so sprightly and amusing that they kept the company in one roar of merry laughter. The

Wizard had trained these pets to do many curious things, and they were so little and so cunning and soft that Polychrome loved to pick
them up as they passed near her place and
fondle them as if they were kittens.

It was late when the entertainment ended,
and they separated to go to their rooms.

"To-morrow," said Ozma, "my invited guests
will arrive, and you will find among them some
interesting and curious people, I promise you.
The next day will be my birthday, and the festivities will be held on the broad green just outside the gates of the City, where all my people
can assemble without being crowded."

"I hope the Scarecrow won't be late," said
Dorothy, anxiously.

"Oh, he is sure to return to-morrow," answered Ozma. "He wanted new straw to stuff himself with, so he went to the Munchkin Country, where straw is plentiful."

With this the Princess bade her guests good night and went to her own room.

Dorothy Receives the Guests

NEXT morning Dorothy's breakfast was served in her own pretty sitting room, and she sent to invite Polly and the shaggy man to join her and Button-Bright at the meal. They came gladly, and Toto also had breakfast with them, so that the little party that had traveled together to Oz was once more reunited.

No sooner had they finished eating than they heard the distant blast of many trumpets, and the sound of a brass band playing martial music; so they all went out upon the balcony. This was at the front of the palace and overlooked the streets of the City, being higher than the wall that shut in the palace grounds. They saw approaching down the street a band of musicians,

playing as hard and loud as they could, while
the people of the Emerald City crowded the sidewalks and cheered so lustily that they almost
drowned the noise of the drums and horns.

Dorothy looked to see what they were cheering at, and discovered that behind the band was
the famous Scarecrow, riding proudly upon the
back of a wooden Saw-Horse which pranced

along the street almost as gracefully as if it had
been made of flesh. Its hoofs, or rather the ends
of its wooden legs, were shod with plates of solid
gold, and the saddle strapped to the wooden
body was richly embroidered and glittered with
jewels.

As he reached the palace the Scarecrow looked
up and saw Dorothy, and at once waved his

peaked hat at her in greeting. He rode up to the front door and dismounted, and the band stopped playing and went away and the crowds of people returned to their dwellings.

By the time Dorothy and her friends had re-entered her room the Scarecrow was there, and he gave the girl a hearty embrace and shook the hands of the others with his own squashy hands, which were white gloves filled with straw.

The shaggy man, Button-Bright, and Polychrome stared hard at this celebrated person, who was acknowledged to be the most popular and most beloved man in all the Land of Oz.

"Why, your face has been newly painted!" exclaimed Dorothy, when the first greetings were over.

"I had it touched up a bit by the Munchkin farmer who first made me," answered the Scarecrow, pleasantly. "My complexion had become a bit grey and faded, you know, and the paint had peeled off one end of my mouth, so I couldn't talk quite straight. Now I feel like myself again, and I may say without immodesty that my body is stuffed with the loveliest oat-straw in all Oz." He pushed against his chest. "Hear me crunkle?" he asked.

"Yes," said Dorothy; "you sound fine."

Button-Bright was wonderfully attracted by

the strawman, and so was Polly. The shaggy man treated him with great respect, because he was so queerly made.

Jellia Jamb now came to say that Ozma wanted Princess Dorothy to receive the invited guests in the Throne-Room, as they arrived. The Ruler was herself busy ordering the preparations for the morrow's festivities, so she wished her friend to act in her place.

Dorothy willingly agreed, being the only other Princess in the Emerald City; so she went to the great Throne-Room and sat in Ozma's seat, placing Polly on one side of her and Button-Bright on the other. The Scarecrow stood at the left of the throne and the Tin Woodman at the right, while the Wonderful Wizard and the shaggy man stood behind.

The Cowardly Lion and the Hungry Tiger came in, with bright new bows of ribbon on their collars and tails. After greeting Dorothy affectionately the huge beasts lay down at the foot of the throne.

While they waited, the Scarecrow, who was near the little boy, asked:

"Why are you called Button-Bright?"

"Don't know," was the answer.

"Oh yes, you do, dear," said Dorothy. "Tell the Scarecrow how you got your name."

"Papa always said I was bright as a button, so mamma always called me Button-Bright," announced the boy.

"Where is your mamma?" asked the Scarecrow.

"Don't know," said Button-Bright.

"Where is your home?" asked the Scarecrow.

"Don't know," said Button-Bright.

"Don't you want to find your mamma again?" asked the Scarecrow.

"Don't know," said Button-Bright, calmly.

The Scarecrow looked thoughtful.

"Your papa may have been right," he observed; "but there are many kinds of buttons, you see. There are silver and gold buttons, which are highly polished and glitter brightly. There are pearl and rubber buttons, and other kinds, with surfaces more or less bright. But there is still another sort of button which is covered with dull cloth, and that must be the sort your papa meant when he said you were bright as a button. Don't you think so?"

"Don't know," said Button-Bright.

Jack Pumpkinhead arrived, wearing a pair of new white kid gloves; and he brought a birthday present for Ozma consisting of a necklace of pumpkin-seeds. In each seed was set a sparkling carolite, which is considered the rarest and most beautiful gem that exists. The necklace was in a plush case and Jellia Jamb put it on a table with the Princess Ozma's other presents.

Next came a tall, beautiful woman clothed in a splendid trailing gown, trimmed with exquisite lace as fine as cobweb. This was the important Sorceress known as Glinda the Good, who had been of great assistance to both Ozma and Dorothy. There was no humbug about her magic, you may be sure, and Glinda was as kind as she was powerful. She greeted Dorothy most lovingly, and kissed Button-Bright and Polly, and smiled upon the shaggy man, after which Jellia Jamb led the Sorceress to one of the most magnificent rooms of the royal palace and appointed fifty servants to wait upon her.

The next arrival was Mr. H. M. Woggle-Bug, T. E.; the "H. M." meaning Highly Magnified

and the "T. E." meaning Thoroughly Educated. The Woggle-Bug was head professor at the Royal College of Oz, and he had composed a fine Ode in honor of Ozma's birthday. This he wanted to read to them; but the Scarecrow wouldn't let him.

Soon they heard a clucking sound and a chorus of "cheep! cheep!" and a servant threw open the door to allow Billina and her ten fluffy chicks to enter the Throne-Room. As the Yellow Hen marched proudly at the head of her family, Dorothy cried, "Oh, you lovely things!" and ran down from her seat to pet the little yellow downy balls. Billina wore a pearl necklace, and around the neck of each chicken was a tiny gold chain holding a locket with the letter "D" engraved upon the outside.

"Open the lockets, Dorothy," said Billina. The girl obeyed and found a picture of herself in each locket. "They were named after you, my dear," continued the Yellow Hen, "so I wanted all my chickens to wear your picture. Cluck—cluck! come here, Dorothy—this minute!" she cried, for the chickens were scattered and wandering all around the big room.

They obeyed the call at once, and came running as fast as they could, fluttering their fluffy wings in a laughable way.

It was lucky that Billina gathered the little

ones under her soft breast just then, for Tik-tok came in and tramped up to the throne on his flat copper feet.

"I am all wound up and work-ing fine-ly," said the clock-work man to Dorothy.

"I can hear him tick," declared Button-Bright.

"You are quite the polished gentleman," said the Tin Woodman. "Stand up here beside the shaggy man, Tik-tok, and help receive the company."

Dorothy placed soft cushions in a corner for Billina and her chicks, and had just returned to the Throne and seated herself when the playing of the royal band outside the palace announced the approach of distinguished guests.

And my, how they did stare when the High Chamberlain threw open the doors and the visitors entered the Throne-Room!

First walked a gingerbread man, neatly formed and baked to a lovely brown tint. He wore a silk hat and carried a candy cane prettily striped with red and yellow. His shirt-front and cuffs were white frosting, and the buttons on his coat were licorice drops.

Behind the gingerbread man came a child with flaxen hair and merry blue eyes, dressed in white pajamas, with sandals on the soles of its pretty bare feet. The child looked around smiling and thrust its hands into the pockets of the

KING DOUGH, THE HEAD BOOLEYWAG,
AND PARA BRUIN

pajamas. Close after it came a big rubber bear, walking erect on its hind feet. The bear had twinkling black eyes and its body looked as if it had been pumped full of air.

Following these curious visitors were two tall, thin men and two short, fat men, all four dressed in gorgeous uniforms.

Ozma's High Chamberlain now hurried forward to announce the names of the new arrivals, calling out in a loud voice:

"His Gracious and Most Edible Majesty, King Dough the First, Ruler of the Two Kingdoms of Hiland and Loland. Also the Head Booleywag of his Majesty, known as Chick the Cherub, and their faithful friend Para Bruin, the rubber bear."

These great personages bowed low as their names were called, and Dorothy hastened to introduce them to the assembled company. They were the first foreign arrivals, and the friends of Princess Ozma were polite to them and tried to make them feel that they were welcome.

Chick the Cherub shook hands with every one, including Billina, and was so joyous and frank and full of good spirits that John Dough's Head Booleywag at once became a prime favorite.

"Is it a boy or a girl?" whispered Dorothy.

"Don't know," said Button-Bright.

"Goodness me! what a queer lot of people you

are," exclaimed the rubber bear, looking at the assembled company.

"So're you," said Button-Bright, gravely. "Is King Dough good to eat?"

"He's too good to eat," laughed Chick the Cherub.

"I hope none of you are fond of gingerbread," said the King, rather anxiously.

"We should never think of eating our visitors, if we were," declared the Scarecrow; "so please do not worry, for you will be perfectly safe while you remain in Oz."

"Why do they call you Chick?" the Yellow Hen asked the child.

"Because I'm an Incubator Baby, and never had any parents," replied the Head Booleywag.

"My chicks have a parent, and I'm it," said Billina.

"I'm glad of that," answered the Cherub, "because they'll have more fun worrying you than if they were brought up in an Incubator. The Incubator never worries, you know."

King John Dough had brought for Ozma's birthday present a lovely gingerbread crown, with rows of small pearls around it and a fine big pearl in each of its five points. After this had been received by Dorothy with proper thanks and placed on the table with the other presents, the visitors from Hiland and Loland were es-

corted to their rooms by the High Chamberlain.
They had no sooner departed than the band
before the palace began to play again, announc-
ing more arrivals, and as these were doubtless
from foreign parts the High Chamberlain hurried back to receive them in his most official
manner.

Important Arrivals

FIRST entered a band of Ryls from the Happy Valley, all merry little sprites like fairy elves. A dozen crooked Knooks followed from the great Forest of Burzee. They had long whiskers and pointed caps and curling toes, yet were no taller than Button-Bright's shoulder. With this group came a man so easy to recognize and so important and dearly beloved throughout the known world, that all present rose to their feet and bowed their heads in respectful homage, even before the High Chamberlain knelt to announce his name.

"The most Mighty and Loyal Friend of Children, His Supreme Highness—Santa Claus!" said the Chamberlain, in an awed voice.

"Well, well, well! Glad to see you—glad to meet you all!" cried Santa Claus, briskly, as he trotted up the long room.

He was round as an apple, with a fresh rosy face, laughing eyes, and a bushy beard as white as snow. A red cloak trimmed with beautiful ermine hung from his shoulders and upon his back was a basket filled with pretty presents for the Princess Ozma.

"Hello, Dorothy; still having adventures?" he asked in his jolly way, as he took the girl's hand in both his own.

"How did you know my name, Santa?" she replied, feeling more shy in the presence of this immortal saint than she ever had before in her young life.

"Why, don't I see you every Christmas Eve, when you're asleep?" he rejoined, pinching her blushing cheek.

"Oh; do you?"

"And here's Button-Bright, I declare!" cried Santa Claus, holding up the boy to kiss him. "What a long way from home you are; dear me!"

"Do you know Button-Bright, too?" questioned Dorothy, eagerly.

"Indeed I do. I've visited his home several Christmas Eves."

"And do you know his father?" asked the girl.

MERRY RYLS AND CROOKED KNOOKS

"Certainly, my dear. Who else do you suppose brings him his Christmas neckties and stockings?" with a sly wink at the Wizard.

"Then where does he live? We're just crazy to know, 'cause Button-Bright's lost," she said.

Santa laughed and laid his finger aside of his nose as if thinking what to reply. He leaned over and whispered something in the Wizard's ear, at which the Wizard smiled and nodded as if he understood.

Now Santa Claus spied Polychrome, and trotted over to where she stood.

"Seems to me the Rainbow's Daughter is farther from home than any of you," he observed, looking at the pretty maiden admiringly. "I'll have to tell your father where you are, Polly, and send him to get you."

"Please do, dear Santa Claus," implored the little maid, beseechingly.

"But just now we must all have a jolly good time at Ozma's party," said the old gentleman, turning to put his presents on the table with the others already there. "It isn't often I find time to leave my castle, as you know; but Ozma invited me and I just couldn't help coming to celebrate the happy occasion."

"I'm so glad!" exclaimed Dorothy.

"These are my Ryls," pointing to the little sprites squatting around him. "Their business is to paint the colors of the flowers when they bud and bloom; but I brought the merry fellows along to see Oz, and they've left their paint-pots behind them. Also I brought these crooked Knooks, whom I love. My dears, the Knooks are much nicer than they look, for their duty is to water and care for the young trees of the forest, and they do their work faithfully and well. It's hard work, though, and it makes my Knooks crooked and gnarled, like the trees themselves; but their hearts are big and kind, as are the hearts of all who do good in our beautiful world."

"I've read of the Ryls and Knooks," said Dorothy, looking upon these little workers with interest.

Santa Claus turned to talk with the Scarecrow and the Tin Woodman, and he also said a kind word to the shaggy man, and afterward went away to ride the Saw-Horse around the Emerald City. "For," said he, "I must see all the grand sights while I am here and have the chance, and Ozma has promised to let me ride the Saw-Horse because I'm getting fat and short of breath."

"Where are your reindeer?" asked Polychrome.

"I left them at home, for it is too warm for them in this sunny country," he answered. "They're used to winter weather when they travel."

In a flash he was gone, and the Ryls and Knooks with him; but they could all hear the golden hoofs of the Saw-Horse ringing on the marble pavement outside, as he pranced away with his noble rider.

Presently the band played again, and the High Chamberlain announced:

"Her Gracious Majesty, the Queen of Merryland."

They looked earnestly to discover whom this queen might be, and saw advancing up the room an exquisite wax doll, dressed in dainty fluffs and ruffles and spangled gown. She was almost as big as Button-Bright, and her cheeks and mouth and eyebrow were prettily painted in delicate colors. Her blue eyes stared a bit, being of glass, yet the expression upon her Majesty's

face was quite pleasant and decidedly winning.
With the Queen of Merryland were four
wooden soldiers, two stalking ahead of her with
much dignity and two following behind, like a
royal bodyguard. The soldiers were painted in
bright colors and carried wooden guns, and
after them came a fat little man who attracted
attention at once, although he seemed modest
and retiring. For he was made of candy, and
carried a tin sugar-sifter filled with powdered
sugar, with which he dusted himself frequently
so that he wouldn't stick to things if he touched
them. The High Chamberlain had called him
"The Candy Man of Merryland," and Dorothy
saw that one of his thumbs looked as if it had
been bitten off by some one who was fond of
candy and couldn't resist the temptation.

The wax doll Queen spoke prettily to Dorothy
and the others, and sent her loving greetings to
Ozma before she retired to the rooms prepared
for her. She had brought a birthday present
wrapped in tissue paper and tied with pink and
blue ribbons, and one of the wooden soldiers
placed it on the table with the other gifts. But
the Candy Man did not go to his room, because
he said he preferred to stay and talk with the
Scarecrow and Tik-tok and the Wizard and Tin
Woodman, whom he declared the queerest people he had ever met. Button-Bright was glad the

Candy Man stayed in the Throne-Room, because the boy thought this guest smelled deliciously of wintergreen and maple sugar.

The Braided Man now entered the room, having been fortunate enough to receive an invitation to the Princess Ozma's party. He was from a cave halfway between the Invisible Valley and the Country of the Gargoyles, and his hair and whiskers were so long that he was obliged to plait them into many braids that hung to his feet, and every braid was tied with a bow of colored ribbon.

"I've brought Princess Ozma a box of flutters for her birthday," said the Braided Man, earnestly; "and I hope she will like them, for they are the finest quality I have ever made."

"I'm sure she will be greatly pleased," said

Dorothy, who remembered the Braided Man well; and the Wizard introduced the guest to the rest of the company and made him sit down in a chair and keep quiet, for, if allowed, he would talk continually about his flutters.

The band then played a welcome to another set of guests, and into the Throne-Room swept the handsome and stately Queen of Ev. Beside her was young King Evardo, and following them came the entire royal family of five Princesses and four Princes of Ev. The Kingdom of Ev lay just across the Deadly Desert to the North of Oz, and once Ozma and her people had rescued the Queen of Ev and her ten children from the Nome King, who had enslaved them. Dorothy had been present on this adventure, so she greeted the royal family cordially; and all the visitors were delighted to meet the little Kansas girl again. They knew Tik-tok and Billina, too, and the Scarecrow and Tin Woodman, as well as the Lion and Tiger; so there was a joyful reunion, as you may imagine, and it was fully an hour before the Queen and her train retired to their rooms. Perhaps they would not have gone then had not the band begun to play to announce new arrivals; but before they left the great Throne-Room King Evardo added to Ozma's birthday presents a diadem of diamonds set in radium.

The next comer proved to be King Renard of Foxville; or King Dox, as he preferred to be called. He was magnificently dressed in a new feather costume and wore white kid mittens over his paws and a flower in his button-hole and had his hair parted in the middle.

King Dox thanked Dorothy fervently for getting him the invitation to come to Oz, which he had all his life longed to visit. He strutted around rather absurdly as he was introduced to all the famous people assembled in the Throne-Room, and when he learned that Dorothy was a Princess of Oz the Fox King insisted on kneeling at her feet and afterward retired backward—a dangerous thing to do, as he might have stubbed his paw and tumbled over.

No sooner was he gone than the blasts of bugles and clatter of drums and cymbals announced important visitors, and the High Chamberlain assumed his most dignified tone as he threw open the door and said proudly:

"Her Sublime and Resplendent Majesty, Queen Zixi of Ix! His Serene and Tremendous Majesty, King Bud of Noland. Her Royal Highness, the Princess Fluff."

That three such high and mighty royal personages should arrive at once was enough to make Dorothy and her companions grow solemn and assume their best company manners; but

HER MAJESTY, QUEEN ZIXI OF IX

when the exquisite beauty of Queen Zixi met their eyes they thought they had never beheld anything so charming. Dorothy decided that Zixi must be about sixteen years old, but the Wizard whispered to her that this wonderful queen had lived thousands of years, but knew the secret of remaining always fresh and beautiful.

King Bud of Noland and his dainty fair-haired sister, the Princess Fluff, were friends of Zixi, as their kingdoms were adjoining, so they had traveled together from their far-off domains to do honor to Ozma of Oz on the occasion of her birthday. They brought many splendid gifts; so the table was now fairly loaded down with presents.

Dorothy and Polly loved the Princess Fluff the moment they saw her, and little King Bud was so frank and boyish that Button-Bright accepted him as a chum at once and did not want him to go away. But it was after noon now, and the royal guests must prepare their toilets for the grand banquet at which they were to assemble that evening to meet the reigning Princess of this Fairyland; so Queen Zixi was shown to her room by a troop of maidens led by Jellia Jamb, and Bud and Fluff presently withdrew to their own apartments.

"My! what a big party Ozma is going to have," exclaimed Dorothy. "I guess the palace will be chock full, Button-Bright; don't you think so?"

"Don't know," said the boy.

"But we must go to our rooms, pretty soon, to dress for the banquet," continued the girl.

"I don't have to dress," said the Candy Man from Merryland. "All I need do is to dust myself with fresh sugar."

"Tik-tok and I always wear the same suits of clothes," said the Tin Woodman; "and so does our friend the Scarecrow."

"My feathers are good enough for any occasion," cried Billina, from her corner.

"Then I shall leave you four to welcome any new guests that come," said Dorothy; "for Button-Bright and I must look our very best at Ozma's banquet."

"Who is still to come?" asked the Scarecrow.

"Well, there's King Kik-a-bray of Dunkiton, and Johnny Dooit, and the Good Witch of the North. But Johnny Dooit may not get here until late, he's so very busy."

"We will receive them and give them a proper welcome," promised the Scarecrow. "So run along, little Dorothy, and get yourself dressed."

The Grand Banquet

I WISH I could tell you how fine the company was that assembled that evening at Ozma's royal banquet. A long table was spread in the center of the great dining-hall of the palace and the splendor of the decorations and the blaze of lights and jewels was acknowledged to be the most magnificent sight that any of the guests had ever seen.

The jolliest person present, as well as the most important, was of course old Santa Claus; so he was given the seat of honor at one end of the table while at the other end sat Princess Ozma, the hostess.

John Dough, Queen Zixi, King Bud, the Queen of Ev and her son Evardo, and the Queen of Merryland had golden thrones to

sit in, while the others were supplied with beautiful chairs.

At the upper end of the banquet room was a separate table provided for the animals. Toto sat at one end of this table, with a bib tied around his neck and a silver platter to eat from. At the other end was placed a small stand, with a low rail around the edge of it, for Billina and her chicks. The rail kept the ten little Dorothys from falling off the stand, while the Yellow Hen could easily reach over and take her food from her tray upon the table. At other places sat the Hungry Tiger, the Cowardly Lion, the Saw-Horse, the Rubber Bear, the Fox King and the Donkey King; they made quite a company of animals.

At the lower end of the great room was another table, at which sat the Ryls and Knooks who had come with Santa Claus, the wooden soldiers who had come with the Queen of Merryland, and the Hilanders and Lolanders who had come with John Dough. Here were also seated the officers of the royal palace and of Ozma's army.

The splendid costumes of those at the three tables made a gorgeous and glittering display that no one present was ever likely to forget; perhaps there has never been in any part of the world at any time another assemblage of such wonderful people as that which gathered this evening to honor the birthday of the Ruler of Oz.

When all the members of the company were in their places an orchestra of five hundred pieces, in a balcony overlooking the banquet room, began to play sweet and delightful music. Then a door draped with royal green opened, and in came the fair and girlish Princess Ozma, who now greeted her guests in person for the first time.

As she stood by her throne at the head of the banquet table every eye was turned eagerly upon the lovely Princess, who was as dignified as she was bewitching, and who smiled upon all her old and new friends in a way that touched their hearts and brought an answering smile to every face.

Each guest had been served with a crystal goblet filled with lacasa, which is a sort of nectar famous in Oz and nicer to drink than soda-water or lemonade. Santa now made a pretty speech in verse, congratulating Ozma on having a birthday, and asking every one present to drink to the health and happiness of their dearly beloved hostess. This was done with great enthusiasm by those who were made so they could drink at all, and those who could not drink politely touched the rims of their goblets to their lips. All seated themselves at the tables and the servants of the Princess began serving the feast.

I am quite sure that only in Fairyland could such a delicious repast be prepared. The dishes were of precious metals set with brilliant jewels and the good things to eat which were placed upon them were countless in number and of exquisite flavor. Several present, such as the Candy Man, the Rubber Bear, Tik-tok, and the Scarecrow, were not made so they could eat, and the Queen of Merryland contented herself with a small dish of sawdust; but these enjoyed the pomp and glitter of the gorgeous scene as much as did those who feasted.

The Woggle-Bug read his "Ode to Ozma," which was written in very good rhythm and was well received by the company. The Wizard added to the entertainment by making a big

DRINKING THE HEALTH OF PRINCESS OZMA OF OZ

pie appear before Dorothy, and when the little girl cut the pie the nine tiny piglets leaped out of it and danced around the table, while the orchestra played a merry tune. This amused the company very much, but they were even more pleased when Polychrome, whose hunger had been easily satisfied, rose from the table and performed her graceful and bewildering Rainbow Dance for them. When it was ended the people clapped their hands and the animals clapped their paws, while Billina cackled and the Donkey King brayed approval.

Johnny Dooit was present, and of course he proved he could do wonders in the way of eating, as well as in everything else that he undertook to do; the Tin Woodman sang a love song, every one joining in the chorus; and the wooden soldiers from Merryland gave an exhibition of a lightning drill with their wooden muskets; the Ryls and Knooks danced the Fairy Circle; and the Rubber Bear bounced himself all around the room. There was laughter and merriment on every side, and everybody was having a royal good time. Button-Bright was so excited and interested that he paid little attention to his fine dinner and a great deal of attention to his queer companions; and perhaps he was wise to do this, because he could eat at any other time.

The feasting and merrymaking continued until late in the evening, when they separated to meet again the next morning and take part in the birthday celebration, to which this royal banquet was merely the introduction.

The Birthday Celebration

A CLEAR, perfect day, with a gentle breeze and a sunny sky, greeted Princess Ozma as she wakened next morning, the anniversary of her birth. While it was yet early all the city was astir and crowds of people came from all parts of the Land of Oz to witness the festivities in honor of their girl Ruler's birthday.

The noted visitors from foreign countries, who had all been transported to the Emerald City by means of the Magic Belt, were as much a show to the Ozites as were their own familiar celebrities, and the streets leading from the royal palace to the jeweled gates were thronged with men, women, and children to see the procession as it passed out to the green fields where the ceremonies were to take place.

And what a great procession it was!

First came a thousand young girls—the prettiest in the land—dressed in white muslin, with green sashes and hair ribbons, bearing great baskets of red roses. As they walked they scattered these flowers upon the marble pavements, so that the way was carpeted thick with roses for the procession to walk upon.

Then came the Rulers of the four Kingdoms of Oz: the Emperor of the Winkies, the Monarch of the Munchkins, the King of the Quadlings and the Sovereign of the Gillikins, each wearing a long chain of emeralds around his neck to show that he was a vassal of the Ruler of the Emerald City.

Next marched the Emerald City Cornet Band, clothed in green-and-gold uniforms and playing the "Ozma Two-Step." The Royal Army of Oz followed, consisting of twenty-seven officers, from the Captain-General down to the Lieutenants. There were no privates in Ozma's Army because soldiers were not needed to fight battles, but only to look important, and an officer always looks more imposing than a private.

While the people cheered and waved their hats and handkerchiefs, there came walking the Royal Princess Ozma, looking so pretty and sweet that it is no wonder her people love her

so dearly. She had decided she would not ride in her chariot that day, as she preferred to walk in the procession with her favored subjects and her guests. Just in front of her trotted the living Blue Bear Rug owned by old Dyna, which wobbled clumsily on its four feet because there was nothing but the skin to support them, with a stuffed head at one end and a stubby tail at the other. But whenever Ozma paused in her walk the Bear Rug would flop down flat upon the ground for the princess to stand upon until she resumed her progress.

Following the Princess stalked her two enormous beasts, the Cowardly Lion and the Hungry Tiger, and even if the Army had not been there these two would have been powerful enough to guard their mistress from any harm.

Next marched the invited guests, who were loudly cheered by the people of Oz along the road, and were therefore obliged to bow to right and left almost every step of the way. First was Santa Claus, who, because he was fat and not used to walking, rode the wonderful Saw-Horse. The merry old gentleman had a basket of small toys with him, and he tossed the toys one by one to the children as he passed by. His Ryls and Knooks marched close behind him.

Queen Zixi of Ix came after; then John Dough and the Cherub, with the rubber bear named Para Bruin strutting between them on its hind legs; then the Queen of Merryland, escorted by her wooden soldiers; then King Bud of Noland and his sister, the Princess Fluff; then the Queen of Ev and her ten royal children; then the Braided Man and the Candy Man, side by side; then King Dox of Foxville and King Kik-a-bray of Dunkiton, who by this time had become good friends; and finally Johnny Dooit, in his leather apron, smoking his long pipe.

These wonderful personages were not more heartily cheered by the people than were those who followed after them in the procession. Dorothy was a general favorite, and she walked arm in arm with the Scarecrow, who was beloved by all. Then came Polychrome and Button-Bright, and the people loved the Rainbow's pretty Daughter and the beautiful blue-eyed boy as soon as they saw them. The shaggy man in his shaggy new suit attracted much attention because he was such a novelty. With regular steps tramped the machine-man Tik-tok, and there was more cheering when the Wizard of Oz followed in the procession. The Woggle-Bug and Jack Pumpkinhead were next, and behind them Glinda the Sorceress and the Good Witch of the North. Finally came Billina, with her brood of chickens to whom she clucked anxiously to keep them together and to hasten them along so they would not delay the procession.

Another band followed, this time the Tin Band of the Emperor of the Winkies, playing a beautiful march called, "There's No Plate like Tin." Then came the servants of the Royal Palace, in a long line, and behind them all the people joined the procession and marched away through the emerald gates and out upon the broad green.

Here had been erected a splendid pavilion, with a grandstand big enough to seat all the royal party and those who had taken part in the procession. Over the pavilion, which was of green silk and cloth of gold, countless banners waved in the breeze. Just in front of this, and connected with it by a runway, had been built a broad platform, so that all the spectators could see plainly the entertainment provided for them.

The Wizard now became Master of Ceremonies, as Ozma had placed the conduct of the performance in his hands. After the people had all congregated about the platform and the royal party and the visitors were seated in the grandstand, the Wizard skillfully performed some feats of juggling glass balls and lighted candles. He tossed a dozen or so of them high in the air and caught them one by one as they came down, without missing any.

Then he introduced the Scarecrow, who did a sword-swallowing act that aroused much interest. After this the Tin Woodman gave an exhibition of Swinging the Axe, which he made to whirl around him so rapidly that the eye could scarcely follow the motion of the gleaming blade. Glinda the Sorceress then stepped upon the platform, and by her magic made a big tree grow in the middle of the space, made blossoms appear upon the tree, and made the blossoms become delicious fruit called tamornas; and so great was the quantity of fruit thus produced that when the servants climbed the tree and tossed it down to the crowd, there was enough to satisfy every person present.

Para Bruin, the rubber bear, climbed to a limb of the big tree, rolled himself into a ball, and dropped to the platform, whence he bounded up again to the limb. He repeated this bouncing act several times, to the great delight of all the children present. After he had finished, and bowed, and returned to his seat, Glinda waved her wand and the tree disappeared; but its fruit still remained to be eaten.

The Good Witch of the North amused the people by transforming ten stones into ten birds, the ten birds into ten lambs, and the ten lambs into ten little girls, who gave a pretty dance and were then transformed into ten stones again,

just as they were in the beginning.

Johnny Dooit next came on the platform with his tool-chest, and in a few minutes built a great flying machine; then put his chest in the machine and the whole thing flew away together—Johnny and all—after he had bid good-bye to those present and thanked the Princess for her hospitality.

The Wizard then announced the last act of all, which was considered really wonderful. He had invented a machine to blow huge soap-bubbles, as big as balloons, and this machine was hidden under the platform so that only the rim of the big clay pipe to produce the bubbles showed above the flooring. The tank of soapsuds, and the air-pumps to inflate the bubbles, were out of sight beneath, so that when the bubbles began to grow upon the floor of the platform it really seemed like magic to the people of Oz, who knew nothing about even the common soap-bubbles that our children blow with a penny clay pipe and a basin of soap-and-water.

The Wizard had invented another thing. Usually soap-bubbles are frail and burst easily, lasting only a few moments as they float in the air; but the Wizard added a sort of glue to his soapsuds, which made his bubbles tough; and, as the glue dried rapidly when exposed to the air, the Wizard's bubbles were strong enough to float for hours without breaking.

He began by blowing—by means of his machinery and air-pumps—several large bubbles which he allowed to float upward into the sky, where the sunshine fell upon them and gave them iridescent hues that were most beautiful. This aroused much wonder and delight, because it was a new amusement to every one present— except perhaps Dorothy and Button-Bright, and even they had never seen such big, strong bubbles before.

The Wizard then blew a bunch of small bubbles and afterward blew a big bubble around them so they were left in the center of it; then he allowed the whole mass of pretty globes to float into the air and disappear in the far distant sky.

"That is really fine!" declared Santa Claus, who loved toys and pretty things. "I think, Mr. Wizard, I shall have you blow a bubble around me; then I can float away home and see the country spread out beneath me as I travel. There isn't a spot on earth that I haven't visited, but I usually go in the night-time, riding behind my swift reindeer. Here is a good chance to observe

THE WIZARD BLEW A BUBBLE AROUND
SANTA CLAUS

the country by daylight, while I am riding slowly and at my ease."

"Do you think you will be able to guide the bubble?" asked the Wizard.

"Oh yes; I know enough magic to do that," replied Santa Claus. "You blow the bubble, with me inside of it, and I'll be sure to get home in safety."

"Please send me home in a bubble, too!" begged the Queen of Merryland.

"Very well, madam; you shall try the journey first," politely answered old Santa.

The pretty wax doll bade good-bye to the Princess Ozma and the others, and stood on the platform while the Wizard blew a big soap-bubble around her. When completed he allowed the bubble to float slowly upward, and there could be seen the little Queen of Merryland standing in the middle of it and blowing kisses from her fingers to those below. The bubble took a southerly direction, quickly floating out of sight.

"That's a very nice way to travel," said Princess Fluff. "I'd like to go home in a bubble, too."

So the Wizard blew a big bubble around Princess Fluff, and another around King Bud, her brother, and a third one around Queen Zixi; and soon these three bubbles had mounted into the sky and were floating off in a group in the direction of the kingdom of Noland.

The success of these ventures induced the other guests from foreign lands to undertake bubble journeys, also; so the Wizard put them one by one inside his bubbles, and Santa Claus directed the way they should go, because he knew exactly where everybody lived.

Finally Button-Bright said:

"I want to go home, too."

"Why, so you shall!" cried Santa; "for I'm sure your father and mother will be glad to see you again. Mr. Wizard, please blow a big, fine bubble for Button-Bright to ride in, and I'll agree to send him home to his family as safe as safe can be."

"I'm sorry," said Dorothy with a sigh, for she was fond of her little comrade; "but p'raps it's best for Button-Bright to get home; 'cause his folks must be worrying just dreadful."

She kissed the boy, and Ozma kissed him, too, and all the others waved their hands and said good-bye and wished him a pleasant journey.

"Are you glad to leave us, dear?" asked Dorothy, a little wistfully.

"Don't know," said Button-Bright.

He sat down cross-legged on the platform, with his sailor hat tipped back on his head, and the Wizard blew a beautiful bubble all around him.

A minute later it had mounted into the sky, sailing toward the west, and the last they saw of Button-Bright he was still sitting in the middle of the shining globe and waving his sailor hat at those below.

"Will you ride in a bubble, or shall I send you and Toto home by means of the Magic Belt?" the Princess asked Dorothy.

"Guess I'll use the Belt," replied the little girl. "I'm sort of 'fraid of those bubbles."

"Bow-wow!" said Toto, approvingly. He loved to bark at the bubbles as they sailed away, but he didn't care to ride in one.

Santa Claus decided to go next. He thanked Ozma for her hospitality and wished her many happy returns of the day. Then the Wizard blew a bubble around his chubby little body and smaller bubbles around each of his Ryls and Knooks.

As the kind and generous friend of children mounted into the air the people all cheered at the top of their voices, for they loved Santa Claus dearly; and the little man heard them through the walls of the bubble and waved his hands in return as he smiled down upon them. The band played bravely while every one

"GOOD-BYE, OZMA! GOOD-BYE, DOROTHY!"

watched the bubble until it was completely out of sight.

"How 'bout you, Polly?" Dorothy asked her friend. "Are you 'fraid of bubbles, too?"

"No," answered Polychrome, smiling; "but Santa Claus promised to speak to my father as he passed through the sky. So perhaps I shall get home an easier way."

Indeed, the little maid had scarcely made this speech when a sudden radiance filled the air, and while the people looked on in wonder the end of a gorgeous rainbow slowly settled down upon the platform.

With a glad cry the Rainbow's Daughter sprang from her seat and danced along the curve of the bow, mounting gradually upward, while the folds of her gauzy gown whirled and floated around her like a cloud and blended with the colors of the rainbow itself.

"Good-bye, Ozma! Good-bye, Dorothy!" cried a voice they knew belonged to Polychrome; but now the little maiden's form had melted wholly into the rainbow, and their eyes could no longer see her.

Suddenly the end of the rainbow lifted and its colors slowly faded like mist before a breeze. Dorothy sighed deeply and turned to Ozma.

"I'm sorry to lose Polly," she said; "but I guess

she's better off with her father; 'cause even the Land of Oz couldn't be like home to a cloud fairy."

"No, indeed," replied the Princess; "but it has been delightful for us to know Polychrome for a little while, and—who knows?—perhaps we may meet the Rainbow's Daughter again, some day."

The entertainment being now ended, all left the pavilion and formed their gay procession back to the Emerald City again. Of Dorothy's recent traveling companions only Toto and the shaggy man remained, and Ozma had decided to allow the latter to live in Oz for a time, at least. If he proved honest and true she promised to let him live there always, and the shaggy man was anxious to earn this reward.

They had a nice quiet dinner together and passed a pleasant evening with the Scarecrow, the Tin Woodman, Tik-tok, and the Yellow Hen for company.

When Dorothy bade them good-night she kissed them all good-bye at the same time. For Ozma had agreed that while Dorothy slept she and Toto should be transported by means of the Magic Belt to her own little bed in the Kansas farm-house and the little girl laughed as she thought how astonished Uncle Henry and

Aunt Em would be when she came down to breakfast with them next morning.

Quite content to have had so pleasant an adventure, and a little tired by all the day's busy scenes, Dorothy clasped Toto in her arms and lay down upon the pretty white bed in her room in Ozma's royal palace.

Presently she was sound asleep.

THE END